CW01474902

The Lighthouse Cafe

GULF COAST GETAWAY BOOK ONE

BEBE REED

LADYBUGBOOKS LLC

Bebe Reed

THE LIGHTHOUSE CAFE

Gulf Coast Getaway
Book 1

CHAPTER 1

Ginny

Virginia Rigby—Ginny, to those who knew her—did not awaken the morning of September fourteenth knowing that her life would change forever.

But it did.

It had already changed three times that she could easily recall. The first was when she married Jack, the second occurred when she gave birth to her first daughter, Chandler, and the third happened when Jack dropped dead from a heart attack just two months prior.

She leaned over and inhaled the exquisite fragrance of the stargazer lilies perched atop her foyer table. Flowers always put her at peace, and she prayed for a calm soul as she stood in the Buckhead house that she had lived in for twenty years.

Jack had bought the home in the wealthy suburbs of Atlanta when the girls were young, after he had started making real money, as he had put it.

A shadow crept up beside her. "The hors d'oeuvres are in the office, ma'am."

"Thank you, Clara."

It had seemed silly for Ginny to request there be hors d'oeuvres at the reading of Jack's will. But to her Southern sensibilities, even a will reading was entertaining guests, and guests must be fed.

1

Clara had done as she asked, of course. Clara always did. She was sublimely loyal in that way.

They had buried Jack in a plot that she had picked out. His heart had been weak for a long time, but Ginny never thought that she'd lose him so quickly, so without notice. Chandler had come down from New York for the funeral, and Reece had flown up from Tulane.

But as soon as he was beneath the ground, Ginny had insisted the girls get back to their lives. After all, Chandler was busy with her jewelry design studio, and Reece was in her second year of medical school.

They didn't need to sit around the agonizingly empty mansion to mope and cry.

Her gaze roved the home that she knew so well. Paintings and Oriental rugs draped the house, unapologetically telling the story of their lives. Jack had been poor when they met. But he'd had a fire that Ginny loved. She'd worked menial jobs while he knocked on doors of financial institutions, begging someone to give him a chance as a broker.

After he finally got his big break and the money started rolling in, he was generous in some ways and not so much in others. Ginny always had an allowance that included the grocery money and wardrobe spending. But keeping up with the other lavishly wealthy wives had always been difficult, if not impossible.

While her husband had splurged on golf memberships, she'd shopped consignment for herself. The items had been upscale, but Ginny's clothes were very rarely ever new.

With Jack's demise, she wouldn't know what to do with the money that was to be inherited.

Dane's head popped out from the parlor. "We're nearly ready."

She pushed up a smile. "Coming."

She checked her appearance in a gilded hallway mirror. Her dark hair had been touched up last week. Her walnut-colored eyes peeked out from bangs that hid the fine lines that ran across her forehead. Oh sure, she could've suffered through Botox like all the other wives. But there was something beautiful about her aged face, or so Ginny like to delude herself in thinking.

The doorbell rang and Clara moved to answer it. A woman with long blonde hair that cascaded down her back entered. She'd been at the funeral with a teenaged son.

Ginny hadn't met her then, but the woman must have been some relative of Jack's that she couldn't remember.

"I'm Ginny." She extended her hand. "I don't think we've met."

The woman's bright blue eyes slashed left. "Savannah."

"Pleased to meet you."

Savannah's gaze bobbed awkwardly around, and Ginny understood. The austerity of the home often intimidated people. Well, she wanted everyone to feel welcome in her house.

"How did you know Jack?" she asked.

Dane's head appeared again. "We're starting."

Just when she was going to find out who the mystery woman was, too. "Be right there." She pulled Savannah's arm gently. "We've been summoned. Best to get this over with. We'll talk after the reading. How's that?"

Savannah made a choking sound and nodded.

The office was a beautiful room with dark oak panels and a glossy marble-topped fireplace. Clara had stationed the food against the wall. It sat near the desk that Dane hovered behind.

Though Ginny had no appetite, she eyed the morsels Clara had beautifully constructed—small quiches, bacon-wrapped dates, a skillet coffee cake cut into bite-sized squares.

At one time she had cooked for Jack—in the early years of their marriage. Her grandmother had willed her the very cookbook that she had constructed meals from, meals that she had often helped stir and whisk when she was a girl.

The book itself was old, created by the local women's club. Ginny had made several of the recipes and had wanted to dig into more of them, but Jack complained they were full of butter and they would make him fat. He insisted they eat lighter, healthier.

So she had put the cookbook in the back of her closet, even though at the time she'd desperately wanted to try her hand at Coca-Cola cake or West Indies Crab Salad.

Now she had all the time in the world to cook and no other skills besides being a housewife. Good thing Jack had left everything to her.

Just before she turned away from the hors d'oeuvres table, another delight snagged her gaze—small stuffed pastries.

She peered at the printed label displayed beneath the silver chafing dish—crab puffs. Jack had despised crab, and so it was always off the menu. But Clara knew that Ginny loved it, and so she had made the puffs for her.

She wasn't sure if Clara serving them was more of a pledge to Ginny or a rebuke of Jack. Her housekeeper had never said as much, but she had long suspected that Clara had disliked her deceased husband.

Well, given that this was the will reading, Ginny wanted to be respectful, which meant that she wouldn't touch the puffs.

Her loyalty lay more with her dead husband, whom she'd been married to for over twenty years, than with her living housekeeper.

Blood always came higher on the priority list.

"Let's get started." Dane cleared his throat. "Is everyone ready?"

Other than Ginny and Savannah, there were only a couple of other people in attendance—Jack's sister, who had never liked Ginny, and her two children, whom Ginny adored.

Dane had been in Jack's fraternity pledge class down at Auburn. After graduating, both men had moved to Atlanta, but every fall football season the couples reunited on weekends to enjoy the seating passes that Jack had purchased for all of them. The seats cost a small fortune, so Ginny made sure they attended as many games as possible to cheer on the Tigers.

It was no surprise that Dane had been the Rigby's family attorney. Jack trusted Dane with everything.

He spoke in a commanding voice. "To my sister, I leave my Jaguar. To the boys, I am leaving trusts."

She barely listened as Dane discussed trusts left for both their girls. She knew all of this. She wondered how empty the house would feel. Should she downsize? But what about all their furnishings? There were so many couches, lamps, paintings, rugs. What would she do with it all?

No. Keep it. The girls would eventually marry, and they would need things. Chandler was practically engaged as it was. She would need to furnish her own home or large apartment soon enough. Ginny could provide the staples. It would make her happy to do so.

"And to Ginny—"

At the mention of her name, she perked up, paying attention.

"To my wife of twenty-eight years—you have been an *accomplished* wife and mother."

4

Accomplished? What a strange word. It was cold, sterile, suggesting more that she was proficient at a sport, at the top of her bowling league, perhaps, than it suggested she'd been an exemplary partner.

Dane continued. "Ginny, I am leaving you money. But I want you to know, and it is not lost on me how much of a shock this will be—but you are not the only woman in my life."

She tugged her ear. "What was that?"

But he didn't stop. "I have a second family. For years they have lived in the shadows, but upon my death, I want them to be known as mine. Because they have had to suffer in silence, from this day forward, the home and everything in it, including all my assets, belong to Savannah Probst and her son—*my* son, William."

She felt all the blood run from her face and into her feet. That name —*Savannah*. It sounded so familiar.

Every gaze in the room landed on her. She felt their stares in the form of pinpricks dancing on her skin. That was the moment when Ginny realized who Savannah was—the woman who'd been at the funeral, the one she had welcomed into her home.

It was the woman sitting right beside her.

Ginny jumped from her chair as if it was aflame. It teetered and crashed to the floor. She stared at Savannah and felt the blood rush back to her cheeks, felt hot anger in the form of stinging flesh.

"You..." she managed in an accusing voice. "You are... Jack did..." Her racing mind settled, and she flipped her stare to the man behind the desk. "Dane, what is the meaning of this? What are you talking about?"

He removed his frameless glasses and rested them on the paper. He rubbed a hand down his face, and Ginny realized that he had known about *that woman*.

And he'd never said a word.

"I know this is a shock."

"A shock?" She was making a scene. Ginny wasn't supposed to do that. Good Southern women didn't make scenes. They smiled and nodded, asked guests if they needed a refreshment. They kept their calm and cool.

But the shock of this information had shattered her calm. How could she be calm when her blood was on fire?

"This isn't a shock, Dane. This is a *scandal*. Jack...how could he have

5

done this? I don't understand!" A bit of sense smashed into her, and she whirled on Savannah. "You! Get out of my house!"

"I'm afraid it isn't your home anymore," Dane said calmly.

She turned to him for sympathy, for help. "You can't be serious. This is my house."

"Not according to the will, it isn't." He lifted the paper and let it fall listlessly back onto the desk. "From the time it is announced that this property belongs to Ms. Probst, meaning right now, you have exactly one hour to vacate the premises."

The world started to spin. The corners of her vision darkened. Adrenaline shot through her veins. This was fight-or-flight. Ginny recognized it from those biology classes she'd had to take in college. Oh, she'd finished and received a Bachelor of Arts before marrying. But she'd majored in English literature—a useless degree that made her eligible to be nothing more than a secretary, or administrative assistant, as it was referred to. It was the same job, only wrapped up and presented with a pretty little bow.

A strange screeching sound that didn't resemble any kind of word flitted from her throat.

Dane said somberly, "I'm afraid that you have to leave."

"I'm not leaving."

"You have no choice. The sheriff will escort you from the premises after you've had time to pack."

She scoffed. "Time to pack?"

He glanced at his watch. "You've already lost five minutes."

Oh God. This was real. It was happening. Everyone in the room just stared at her as they witnessed her shame. How could Jack have done this to her? To the girls?

All she wanted to do was crumple into a ball, but her lizard brain, the part that focused on survival, kicked in.

"How much money did he leave me?"

Dane pointed to a figure on the paper. The world tilted again, and the floor appeared much closer than Ginny knew it was when she was standing upright.

She got control of herself. "But the house is worth five times that. The assets, even more."

"I'm sorry." He wasn't sorry. If Dane had been sorry, he would've told his old friend that his will was horrible. "I suggest you pack."

Well, Ginny knew one thing—she didn't want to be in that room any longer. Her gaze scraped over the room and landed on Savannah. Her fingers flexed. Part of her wanted to strangle the woman. But Savannah looked lost and uncomfortable. Perhaps she hadn't known how this would all turn out.

"How could you do this?" she asked.

But she didn't wait on an answer. She turned on her heel and raced to her bedroom.

"Clothes, all the clothes."

She grabbed her suitcase, the one she used on overseas trips, and filled it with everything she could think of—tops, bottoms, shoes, furs, jewelry. Yes, get the jewelry. She didn't want that woman to have any of it.

After the jewelry she grabbed pictures. She spotted one of her and Jack with the girls. She picked it up and smashed it against a mirror.

"Oops."

She raced from her bedroom, knowing that she must've spent at least forty minutes going through her things. What would she tell the girls? She was destitute? Living out of her suitcase?

She made her way to the kitchen and spotted the glass-covered cabinets filled with cookbooks she'd never used. The one her grandmother had given sat, fat and yellow, like a ray of sunshine, in the very center. It's cheerful cover beckoned Ginny.

Since Jack was dead, now she'd have time to finally cook all those recipes she'd ignored for thirty years.

She shoved it into her purse and took another glance around the room. She'd built a life in this house. They had raised the girls here. They'd held parties for friends, had engagement parties. Her entire life was tied inside those brick walls.

Now it was gone, vanished. She knew that Jack was sometimes cold and distant, but she never imagined that all his business trips had been spent visiting his second family.

Now his frugalness made sense. He'd had another woman and child to support. Ginny had gotten the short end of the stick during his life, and she was getting it in his death, too.

Clara entered the room carrying a silver tray. "Can I get you anything, Mrs. Rigby?"

In her question came an apology. It wasn't Clara's place to console her, so the next best thing was to offer her comfort in another form.

"What's that a plate of?" she asked.

"The crab puffs."

She eyed the tray hungrily. Though she realized Clara hadn't known what would be revealed during Jack's will, it was almost as if the woman was clairvoyant. She'd spat on his grave just a little bit with that tray.

Ginny appreciated that.

Dane entered the kitchen. "You've got a few more minutes, Ginny."

Ginny, mad from the confusion and incoherence of the past hour, plucked one of the crab puffs from the tray and stuffed it into her mouth.

Dane regarded her like a person did when witnessing a crazy person talking to themselves on a subway platform, by recoiling. "Do you need more time?"

Oh, that crab puff had been delicious. "Clara, you outdid yourself. Dane, no, I won't be needing one minute more."

With that, she grabbed the tray of puffs and left her house, and life, forever.

CHAPTER 2

Ginny

G inny had no idea where she was going. She got into her Mercedes and headed south. She'd considered driving up to New York to see Chandler, but the idea of sitting behind the wheel for fourteen hours didn't sound all that fun.

She couldn't afford the plane ticket, anyway. Oh, the inheritance amount that Dane had shown her seemed like a lot, but once taxes were paid, Ginny would be on a fixed income. There was no doubt about that.

Her second choice was to visit Reece in New Orleans. That sounded much better. She could disappear into the smoky nooks and dark crannies of the French Quarter for a few days. That would give her time to figure out exactly what her next steps would be.

Yes, it was a solid plan.

She attempted to keep her mind occupied while driving, but it was impossible to think of anything besides what her dead husband had done.

How was she going to tell the girls?

With the most dignity she could muster. She would arrive in Tulane and call Chandler and ask her to fly down, and then she'd tell both girls face-to-face.

She'd had always been just a touch closer to Reece than Chandler, and she regretted that now. But her eldest had simply gravitated toward Jack more, and he'd loved lavishing attention on her, buying her gifts every time he went away...*to hide away a second wife and son*, she reminded herself coldly.

If there was a means to keep such terrible news from the girls, then she would do it. But there was no way to explain losing the house without telling them the depths of her shame.

She could only blame herself. Surely Ginny had caused Jack to find another woman. It must've been her fault. Perhaps she hadn't doted on him enough. Perhaps she hadn't been as good a housewife as she thought. Maybe she should have gotten a job once the girls didn't need her as much anymore.

The problem with that were her qualifications—she wasn't fit to do anything except answer a phone.

Or...maybe it was all a mistake. Maybe Jack hadn't meant to take the house from her.

Even as the thought flitted through her mind, she knew that was wrong. He'd confiscated the house to give to his mistress.

Rage like lava flowed through her veins. Who was this woman to steal Ginny's life from her? She would fight the will. Maybe she could win. Didn't she deserve more than that hussy's scraps?

With her head spinning, Ginny decided that she wasn't in any hurry to reach Tulane and headed toward Montgomery. It would take a little longer to reach New Orleans by this route, but she'd stop off at the wonderful gift and confection shop, Priester's Pecans. After all, she didn't have a schedule to keep, and she was all out of crab puffs.

* * *

Priester's was a massive store with everything from T-shirts and collectibles to homemade pecan logs and divinity that was to die for. After drifting through the merchandise, she purchased a steaming-hot plate piled high with baked chicken, comforting butter beans, buttery corn bread and tart cherry cobbler. She gulped sweet tea from a glass filled to the brim with clinking ice and the sugary beverage.

Once she was stuffed, she headed back onto the interstate. The sun was setting, and pink and blue washed across the sky in streaks that should have charmed her but had little effect on this day.

She was getting tired, and shame started burrowing deep in her heart.

An uncertain future loomed in front of her. The gut-wrenching realization that she would have to confess to the girls exactly what had happened made her ache to her bones.

By the time she reached the exchange of I-10, Ginny realized that she simply couldn't go west. She couldn't take the right that would lead her to Tulane and reality.

For *that* moment, in her car, there was no reality. There was no past and no future. She didn't have to accept that she was homeless and would need to buy a house and find a menial job doing goodness knew what just so that she could put food on the table.

So instead of driving to face her future, Ginny turned left on I-10. The beach would be this way, and she always loved the beach.

* * *

She exited the interstate at the signs for Foley and Gulf Shores. The idea of rolling down her windows and letting the salty breeze tangle her hair sounded jubilant.

She had planned to stop for the night in Gulf Shores, but the streets teemed with cars. Tourists skirted across the highway toward bustling seafood restaurants. The town was too busy, with too many tourists, as was usually the case.

She kept driving. Before Ginny knew it, she was in Pensacola and then heading toward Destin and the emerald waters in the Florida Panhandle.

Destin was always a lovely place to stay, but she still had energy, so she kept on.

It was getting late now. The sun had long sunk into the horizon. The sky was inky black and dotted with stars. With every breath of the briny air she felt better, as if the weight of the world was slowly easing from her shoulders.

As she kept the Mercedes pointed east, the buildings began getting farther and farther apart. Suddenly fatigue was overtaking her. She was so, so tired, she thought that she'd just pull over for a moment and get out, stretch her legs.

She passed a sign for Mexico Beach and pulled her car over onto the shoulder a little way out of town. There was a long stretch of beach to her right, and she left her vehicle to walk on that strip of white sand.

It was heaven to feel the sugary substance sink between her toes and to really breathe in the salty air, to fill her lungs to bursting and exhale fully.

Ginny promised herself that she would only stay a few minutes and then she'd be gone. She would get back in her car and go to New Orleans to face her new life, however uncertain it was.

After a few minutes listening to the sound of the dark waves as they crashed against the beach and feeling the breeze pick up her hair and toss it into a beautiful mess, she returned to her car.

As soon as her body slumped onto the seat, fatigue overtook her. Her body had been surging with adrenaline most of the day, and it was finally settling down.

As her eyelids shut, she thought that a few minutes wouldn't hurt anything.

The next thing she knew, sunlight was piercing the windshield and someone was tapping on her driver's side window.

She jerked back as a policeman towered over her Mercedes. The man removed his dark sunglasses and said in a powerful tone, "Ma'am, I need you to exit the vehicle. Right now."

CHAPTER 3

Ginny

W as she being arrested? Ginny had never so much as suffered a traffic violation. It would just be rich if she got arrested the day after discovering her life was ruined.

She parted her lips and realized that her mouth was drier than parchment. The water bottle that sat in the console only had enough for one more sip.

"Ma'am, please exit the vehicle."

The sunlight stabbed her eyes as she slowly unlocked and pushed open the door. "I'm sorry, Officer. Have I done something wrong?"

"Have you been drinking?"

"Goodness, no. I just..." *Had a nervous breakdown yesterday and drove here* didn't sound like a fantastic response. Besides, where was here? "I'm sorry. I got lost."

His name tag read *Brantley*. Officer Brantley pulled his dark shades off, revealing warm brown eyes that were just a touch more chocolate than his dark hair.

"Are you okay? Do you need me to call someone for you?" he asked, seeming to genuinely be concerned for her. She bitterly thought that this man was more worried about her well-being than her dead husband.

She waved him away. "No, I'll be fine."

Brantley pointed to the left, and that was when Ginny realized that she'd parked right across the street from a local gas station that advertised breakfast.

"The owner called me about a suspicious vehicle, but you don't look all that suspicious."

She laughed. "No, I'm just...me. I promise that I'm not up to any wrongdoing."

"Good. Have a nice day."

He started to leave, and she panicked, realizing that she still didn't know where she was. "Officer?"

He turned. "Yes?"

She couldn't think of anything more embarrassing than having to admit that she no idea where she was. "What town is this?"

"Sugar Cove."

"Sugar Cove?" She had never heard of it, and she'd been to this part of the Panhandle dozens of times. "Where, exactly, is that?"

"Between Mexico Beach and Port St. Joe. It's a small hamlet and quiet, a nice community." He pointed toward the water. "We even have our own tourist spot."

She followed his finger and spotted a road lined with shops. Squished between the shops and towering over the beach stood a tall lighthouse.

"It's going on auction today," he told her. "But you can tour it for free right now."

"What's going up for auction?"

"The Sugar Cove Lighthouse."

"For sale?"

"Yep. Have a great day," he said before disappearing inside his cruiser.

She found herself at a total loss as to what to do. Her stomach rumbled, and she could go for an iced coffee. Even though it was September, the sun was already frying her skin. It couldn't hurt to walk around for a few minutes and stretch out the kink that had nestled itself between her shoulders. Then she'd find a hotel, check in and get cleaned up. After that she'd head to Tulane, just like she'd intended.

A young woman with red hair and a smattering of freckles across her nose greeted Ginny when she entered the gas station.

"Morning!"

"I owe y'all an apology as I'm the person who sent this place into a tizzy," Ginny admitted bashfully.

"You didn't upset anything." An older woman, perhaps in her seventies, waddled from the back wearing a clean white apron and had her hair pulled back into a bun. "We just wanted to make sure that you were okay. I'm Vera Thompson and this is my granddaughter, Shelby."

"Ginny Rigby. I'm just passing through," she said lightly. "But I was hoping you might have coffee."

"Both hot and iced," Shelby confirmed.

She near fell to her knees in happiness. "I'll have some iced. Where do you keep it?"

"I make it," Shelby said. "Cream?"

"Please." No point in worrying about calories now. She had no one to look beautiful for.

While Shelby built her coffee, she took a moment to absorb her surroundings. The gas station had a breakfast counter to order from and a few booths covered in shiny brown vinyl to enjoy a meal in. Though the seats were worn, they were clean.

Along the walls were shelved the usual convenience foods that filled all roadside watering holes, but there was more to it than that. The station specialized in breakfast wraps. Ginny might've grabbed one if she hadn't filled up on so much junk food the day before. She was still full of all that.

She used the bathroom to freshen up, and by the time she had reached the counter again, her coffee was ready.

"Thank you," she said.

"You here to check out the lighthouse?" Vera asked, eyeing her curiously from behind the food counter.

"No, I don't think so."

Intrigue sparked in Shelby's eyes. "The place hasn't been open in ages. The last owner ran a restaurant inside, but that was years ago. She also lived there. But then she shut down the restaurant and became a hermit. Hardly ever left. No one's seen the inside of the place in at least five years."

"More like a decade," Vera announced with authority.

"What happened to her? Why'd she become a hermit?"

Vera shrugged her broad shoulders. "Dementia, I think, but no one ever really said. Anyway, the place is going up for auction today. Wonder what state it's in."

"It wouldn't surprise me if there were cobwebs to the ceiling," Shelby added. "Not that I'm trying to gossip. I don't mean to sound like I am."

This little place Sugar Cove was different than most of Florida, or at least the busy places that she had visited. Both Shelby and Vera had distinct Southern accents. You didn't find that often in the Panhandle. Though Florida was technically part of the South, it was its own state, with most of the residents being transplants from the north.

But Sugar Cove seemed like a tiny slice of the South built just down from Mexico Beach.

"Y'all have accents."

"We do. A lot of the residents here do," Vera confided while stirring what looked like grits in a pan. "We're mostly local folks, born and raised. We stay put and don't move off much."

"I see." She sipped her coffee. It was a perfect blend of strong beans and thick cream. It was heaven and exactly what she needed. "Thank you."

"Be sure to check out the lighthouse," Vera called as she exited the door.

The sun was climbing high into the sky when she stepped outside. The bike path that ran alongside the road was busy with folks all streaming toward the lighthouse. She had never been inside one, so she figured that she might as well peek. Then she'd leave. She'd head off and start her new life doing whatever it was she was supposed to do when a person woke up to find their entire existence had been yanked out beneath them like a proverbial rug.

People said, "Good morning," as she made her way down the path. She greeted them as well and was surprised when she reached the lighthouse to find that it had an exterior brick building attached to it. That must've been where the restaurant and sleeping quarters were located.

She followed the line of people inside the house and found it bright and cheery. The first room she entered was covered in paneling that was painted light lemon. Several windows were sprinkled about, allowing plenty of light to enter the room.

Ginny instantly imagined how the space could've been the main dining room of a restaurant. It was welcoming and friendly.

She found herself smiling as she followed the winding line of people through the kitchen. There were a couple of large appliances with doors

—refrigerator and freezer, more than likely. There was also a four-burner stove and a small flat grill. The woman who'd owned the restaurant had kept all the appliances. She could just imagine standing in front of the burner, making meals. She could also envision several small round tables with cane-backed chairs in the dining room. Perhaps the tables would be covered in red-and-white-checkered cloths.

She nearly laughed out loud at how silly she was being. The restaurant days of the lighthouse were long gone.

Next she traveled into the master bedroom. It was small and cozy, the walls there painted a soft blue. The plaster crumbled in places, revealing brick beneath it. How lovely it would be with the plaster removed and the brick painted directly.

The bathroom beside the bedroom was small, with dated flamingo-pink tile. But anything could be changed in a place if the bones were good.

From what she saw, the bones of the lighthouse were very, very good indeed.

She entered another bedroom and then walked through an enclosed breezeway that connected the lighthouse to the main living quarters. Plenty of people were climbing the stairs that led to the top of the tower, and she started to, but the brick was too close, the staircase too dark.

Her heart bounded around in her chest, and she took a deep breath and turned around, colliding with a body.

"You okay there?" asked a man, his Southern drawl rich and his voice velvety.

"Sorry," she murmured, glancing up briefly into eyes of the deepest blue. "I don't like tight spaces."

His fingers grazed her arm. "Can I help you down?"

"No." She pulled her arm away and touched her forehead. "I'm fine, thank you."

She made her way back to the front room, where chairs were being placed. People started filling them, signifying that the auction was about to begin. How exciting. Ginny wanted to see who would buy this charming lighthouse.

Would the buyer want to live in such a place? Or would they turn it into a museum, or restore the restaurant? The house intrigued her, and even though she hadn't walked the stairs to the top, Ginny could imagine how glorious the view was from there, how it would span the emerald coast. The waters in this part of Florida were a vibrant green-blue, the sand like white sugar, soft and billowy.

Before she could stop herself, she sat in an empty seat.

A few moments later someone sat beside her. It was the man she'd collided with.

"Sorry about earlier," she murmured.

"As long as you're okay now," he said.

He had salt-and-pepper hair and deep crows' feet that kissed the corners of his eyes. He looked as if he spent every day on the beach, soaking in the easy life that the gulf had to offer.

Before she could stop herself, she leaned over. "Does it work? The lighthouse?"

Why was she even asking it? In an hour she would be gone, on the road to Tulane.

He replied in a conspiratorial tone, "It might." As a blush crept onto her cheeks, he added in a kind voice, "No, the light hasn't worked in years, not once it was decommissioned by the government."

For some reason she thought that depressing. "Could it? Could the new owner start it again?"

"I don't know," he replied. "Did you come to bid on it?"

She scoffed. "No. I'm just passing through." She drank in the surroundings. "But it does have charm."

"And history," he told her.

"I bet." She found herself smiling. Even though she was broken on the inside, cracked in two, being in the lighthouse eased her brokenness slightly. There was still a lot more to be fixed, but a small sliver of happiness was better than nothing.

Before she could ask about the history of the place, the auctioneer announced that they would start the bidding at two hundred thousand dollars.

That was all? Two hundred thousand? It was a steal for a place on the beach in a small hamlet that was as lovely as the two towns that flanked it.

"Does anyone want to start?" the auctioneer asked.

A man down front did. "Two hundred twenty-five."

"That's a steal," she whispered to the stranger beside her.

"You should bid," he whispered.

"No," she said dismissively.

But what if she did? And then, as if her mouth was acting of its own accord, she found herself calling out, "Two hundred and fifty thousand."

The man down the way upped it to three hundred. Ginny topped him at three twenty-five. The man shook his head. That was as high as he was willing to go.

What was she doing? Was she really buying a lighthouse? What would she do with it?

Before another thought entered her head, the stranger said, "Three hundred and fifty thousand."

She stared at him. Why was he bidding?

He winked. "Your turn." *Her turn?* They were bidding against one another? "Better grab it or else I will."

He'd said it as a joke, but this man didn't know what she had been through in the past twenty-four hours. After having so much taken from her, she was not about to let this lighthouse be snatched from her grasp as well.

It was insane, she knew. She had no plan, no idea what to do with the place, but when she glanced around those four walls and spied the beach and water through the windows, Ginny knew that she had to have the place.

She kept bidding, and so did the stranger. Every time she threw out a number, he topped her. The crowd stared at both of them, two people side by side, one-upping the other.

"Five hundred thousand," he said.

People shook their heads. It wasn't worth it, they were silently saying. The stranger smiled at her as if he had her. There was no way that she would go any higher, that's what the look on his face said.

But she had nothing to lose. And so she gave one last bid, one last amount, and it was just shy of everything that Jack had left her. She didn't want the money anyway. What would she do with it in the bank? Stare at it? No, if he had wanted her to make a new life, she would.

When the stranger didn't top her final bid, the auctioneer slammed a gavel onto the lectern in front of him. "Sold! The lighthouse belongs to the lovely lady in the back. Congratulations!"

As elated as Ginny was, she thought that she might just throw up.

What had she done?

CHAPTER 4

Ginny

What had she done?

The stranger gave her a wink and a warm, "Congratulations," before rising and leaving the lighthouse.

It felt like the ground was falling away from her feet, that she had been duped into making a purchase she hadn't wanted.

But the thing was, she did want the lighthouse.

Before she had too much time to think and decide to back out of her decision, a flurry of paperwork was thrust upon her, and a wire transfer was requested. She would have to call Dane to get the funds.

Oh goodness. She'd purchased property at auction in a town where she didn't know a soul. Not one person.

But Ginny took it in stride as any Southern lady would. She filled out the paperwork and then made the dreaded call.

"Dane, I need my inheritance from Jack. Right now," she insisted.

Dane sputtered. "You know it's going to take time to push all of that through."

She ground her teeth together. "I don't care what you must do, what favors you have to call in. I need that money in my account today."

"Why the rush?"

She lifted her chin and felt a surge of confidence. "I'm starting my new life. Because that's what Jack wanted, right? For me to begin anew. If I'm going to get it going right, I need that money."

Dane was silent for a moment. "Jack never intended for you to do something rash."

"Didn't he? He up and handed my home—*my home*—to his hussy and their illegitimate child, but he didn't expect me to do anything rash? What do you think he wanted me to do, buy the house next door and attend to his mistress?"

"Now, Ginny—"

She cut Dane off before he said something stupid that he would later regret, like about how Jack hadn't meant to hurt her. "I don't care what you have to do, but make sure that money is in my account by lunchtime and not a second later. Or else you'll be hearing from my own lawyer."

Not that she had one, but he didn't know that. After she hung up the phone, Ginny set about finishing her purchase of one Sugar Cove Lighthouse.

* * *

Dane had wired the money. He had probably been forced to send it from his own account. It didn't matter to her where it had come from, but nearly every last dime of it had gone to purchasing the property. Now that she had it, what would she do with it?

Ginny sat atop the bed. All the furnishings had been left, which was a good thing. She had gotten dinner from the gas station across the road. Vera had been overjoyed to hear she'd purchased the lighthouse. But her earlier elation, the initial head rush of it all was fading fast.

Now the dread was settling in.

To ease her discomfort, she started unpacking. She put away the silks and leather, the furs. Now she didn't want any of it. It didn't fit beach life.

Neither did she.

As she finished storing the last of her belongings, she came across the faded cookbook. Her mother had gifted Ginny *her* mother's cookbook on the day she married Jack.

She peeled back the cover and read the inscription.

Virginia,

I hope this cookbook brings as much happiness to you and Jack as it did to your father and me.
Love,
Mama

If only her mother had known that Ginny only created a handful of recipes before Jack complained about the fattiness of them all.

She sighed. Well, now she had all the time in the world to cook.

Her phone rang and fear instantly sprang into her. What if it was one of the girls? How would she ever explain what she'd done?

But it wasn't. It was her best friend in all the world, Farrah Jernigan.

"Virginia Rigby, I have been calling you all day. Why haven't you picked up?"

It warmed Ginny's heart how much Farrah loved her. They'd been best friends since she first moved to Buckhead, as Farrah wasn't stuffy like many of the old-money wives. She didn't take life too seriously, and though she was fabulously wealthy, Farrah would've gladly given anyone her fortune. She was simply a generous person.

Ginny sighed. "I'm sorry that I didn't phone. I've been busy."

"All of Buckhead is talking. Are you okay? I heard some hussy moved into your house. What is going on? Tell me everything."

She broke down as she told the entire sordid tale. Farrah cried with her and cursed Jack just like best friends were supposed to.

"Where are you? I'm coming to you."

"I'm sitting in the lighthouse that I purchased today."

"What? No, you didn't."

Ginny lifted her palm. "Hand to heart, I did. And now I regret it. It's just, the place used to be a restaurant, and it's so charming, and it was up for auction, and I couldn't help myself."

"Okay, first off, Virginia Rigby, you are the gutsiest person I know. Secondly, where the heck are you?"

"Sugar Cove. It's between Mexico Beach and Port St. Joe."

"Oh, I love that area. I'll be there tomorrow."

"Wait. What? You can't come here."

Farrah scoffed. "And why not? You need a friend right now and I'm not going to take no for an answer. You've gone and bought yourself a lighthouse. Who's going to help you climb all those stairs and turn the light on at night?"

"It's been decommissioned. It doesn't light anymore. And besides, the tower staircase is very narrow," she added, feeling her throat shrivel at the thought of that claustrophobic space.

Farrah tutted in sympathy. "Well, you don't have to go up in it, I suppose. But I do think you've got to have some kind of light on there. It doesn't have to be bright enough to steer ships, but who's ever heard of a dark lighthouse?"

Ginny supposed no one had. It was a juxtaposition of words, wasn't it? A dark lighthouse simply didn't make sense.

"Fine, you can come tomorrow."

"Is it safe for you to be there alone tonight? Do I need to be worried about you?"

Ginny wondered how on earth she could've *not* called Farrah after being kicked out of her house yesterday. But the shame of the situation still clung to her like the smell of day-old fish.

"You don't need to be worried about me. Come tomorrow. I could use some help figuring things out."

"Great. I'll be there by ten a.m. Think it'll be hard to find the place?"

She laughed. "Just enter town and you'll see the lighthouse on the right. You can't miss it."

"Great. Will do. And Ginny?"

"Yes?"

"What have you told the girls?"

And there, her blood went icy. "I haven't had the heart to tell them anything."

"Okay, we'll come up with a plan tomorrow then. I'm sure one day won't make a difference."

As Ginny hung up the phone, she ignored the tug in the back of her mind to call her daughters. Little did she know, but a single day would make a difference.

It would make a very large one indeed.

CHAPTER 5

Reece

R eece Rigby was failing medical school with style, thank you very much. It wasn't something that she was proud of.

In fact, she was racked with guilt over it. But she told herself that she'd made a 34 on her last cardiovascular exam because of her dad's death.

But that didn't explain why she'd also failed the exam on hematology she'd taken at the end of last year.

Medical school was hard. There was no going around it. Her advisor had already told her to plan on summer school. He'd also suggested that maybe she take some time off. After all, losing your father unexpectedly like she had would throw anyone off their game.

Which was why she was taking the weekend to go home for a surprise visit to her mother. Mama had been through a lot, and she hadn't called after the reading of the will. Reece expected this meant everything had gone to plan. But it was always good to check and make sure.

She pulled into the circular drive at the Buckhead home and released a breath as she sank onto the leather seat of her BMW. It was much too flashy of a vehicle for her. Reece would've rather had an SUV. But her father had said that if he was the one buying the vehicle, then she would take what she got.

She reached for her purse, which was leaning precariously to one side in the seat next to her. When her fingers didn't quite manage to grab hold, the bag tilted, and the contents spilled out.

She scooped up the guts of her purse, palming the ebony ballpoint pen that her father had given her when she was accepted into Tulane's prestigious medical school.

"You'll save many lives with this pen," he'd told her, meaning that she would write prescriptions that would heal and mend.

Sure, she would. If she managed to graduate, that was.

But ever since her father had passed away, Reece had experienced a gnawing in her stomach, like a mouse was trapped inside and was attempting to work its way out.

He'd known she was struggling in school. She'd gone to him at the end of last semester with her doubts about forging into the medical profession.

Her father had looked at her coldly while he sat behind his grand mahogany desk. "You will not fail medical school and bring shame to our family. I'm counting on you. *We're all* counting on you."

But she *had* failed the hematology test, and it was after his stern words that she noticed a change in her father. He seemed frailer, not as active. She'd suspected his heart was acting up and told him to be sure to get his checkup from the cardiologist, but her father had assured her that everything was fine.

A few short months later he was dead, and Reece was stuck thinking about how she'd disappointed him with that grade. Maybe if she'd tried harder, the stress wouldn't have gotten to him and he'd still be alive.

She'd let him down and now he was gone, which meant her mother expected Reece to become the doctor that Jack Rigby had always wanted.

But Reece's heart simply wasn't in it. The ebony pen that she now stuffed into her purse was a reminder of how she had disappointed him. There was only one choice—she could not fail her mother and add to her grief, no matter how much she hated medicine.

She had debated on the drive about telling her mother the results of her last exam, and as she took the brick steps two at a time to the front door, Reece decided not to say one word. Her mother needed her support. She didn't need to be holding her grown daughter's hand. Reece would simply swallow her distaste for school, work hard the rest of the year and fix her grade that summer. End of story.

She pushed her door key into the lock and tried to turn the key, but the lock wouldn't give. "What the—"

She checked to make sure she hadn't accidentally used her apartment key, which she hadn't. So she jiggled the key, but the lock still wouldn't give.

Huffing with annoyance, she rang the doorbell. A moment later a woman with long blonde hair answered. A new friend of her mama's, perhaps?

"Hey, I'm Reece," she said politely. "Ginny's daughter."

She moved to enter, but the woman didn't adjust her stance for her to slip by. In fact, she stepped forward, guarding the entrance like a dragon protecting its lair.

"Ginny doesn't live here anymore," the woman said.

Her eyes narrowed. Surely the woman was off her rocker. "Is this some joke? Did Mama put you up to this?" Reece called out, "Mama, it's me. I'm home!"

She fully expected to hear her light laughter. The sound always reminded Reece of wind chimes being tickled by a breeze. But her mother's voice did not fill the hallway.

"Where's my mama?" she asked the woman.

The woman closed her eyes as if frustrated by her very presence. "I don't know. But if you would like to find out, I suggest you call her."

"I'll just wait here." Reece moved to enter again, because surely this was some sick joke that the woman was playing. Why she would do such a thing so recently after they had lost their father was beside her, but she decided as soon as her mother came home, they would have a word about her new friend.

"Ginny is gone," the woman snapped. "Like I said, she doesn't live here anymore. She has moved out. If you want to find her, call her."

While growing up, Reece was known as the fiery one, the daughter with the temper that could cause gasoline to ignite without a spark. Anger flared in her gut bright and hot.

"This is my home," she yelled, "and if you refuse to let me in, I will call the police." She yanked her cell from her purse for dramatic effect. "Right now."

The blonde woman glanced over her shoulder and seemed content with whatever she heard there. She slipped outside and quietly shut the door behind her.

"I can understand why your mother hasn't called you yet. Everything happened suddenly yesterday. She didn't have time to prepare for it. You need to call and make sure that she's okay."

Reece's mind swam. "Didn't have time to prepare for what? What are you talking about?"

"My name is Savannah Probst."

"Okay," she said, not bothering to hide the I-really-don't-care-who-you-are tone in her voice. "What's that got to do with anything?"

"I can't tell you more, but you need to contact your mother. She's going through some...things."

That Savannah woman made it sound like she was going to jump off a cliff or something. Reece pushed back the dull brown hair that had fallen over her eyes.

"My mama isn't in danger, is she?"

Savannah hesitated. "She's not in danger from me or anyone else, no."

A bitter, disbelieving laugh escaped Reece's throat. "Then who is she in danger from? Ma'am, I think you need to tell me everything that's going on because as of yesterday, this was my home. My childhood things are inside."

"I'll make sure that you get everything that's yours. Now, please leave before I call the police and have you escorted off my property."

The words slammed into her. This woman wasn't kidding. Reece's mother didn't live here anymore. As of yesterday, she was gone. But where to? Was she okay? What in the world was happening?

Before she could ask another question, Savannah slipped back inside the house and quietly shut the door. That was when Reece thumbed her phone to life and started dialing.

CHAPTER 6

Ginny

"I t's wonderful," Farrah cooed, spinning around the front room of the home.

It sat empty now, the auction chairs all swept away. Sunlight streamed through the windows, making the room seem to spill over with coziness from the inside out.

Ginny nibbled the inside of her cheek nervously. "You like it?"

"I love it." Farrah clapped her hands, and a smile wide as a mile splashed over her face. "What are you going to do with it?"

"Here. Let me show you the kitchen."

That morning, before Farrah had arrived, Ginny found time to tinker with the appliances in the grand galley space, which was separated from the front room by two swinging doors with peepholes circled into them.

Farrah nodded in approval. "Good refrigerator and freezer space. Everything's clean. Does it all work?"

She nodded, trying to keep her enthusiasm in check because ideas were swirling. But they seemed too grandiose for a woman who'd spent the past twenty years volunteering for the PTO, being a member of the library board and often entertaining guests.

"It does work," she assured Farrah as she turned the dial that would heat the grill and fiddled with the knobs to the double oven. "I had everything on this morning, and I also had time to make this."

She pulled a clean tea towel she'd discovered among the previous owner's things off the top of a cast-iron skillet. Underneath lay a browned cake, and the scent of cinnamon trickled up Ginny's nose.

"Why, Virginia Rigby," Farrah said, "you found time to entertain?"

"What I *found* was the time to open my grandmother's old cookbook and select the perfect snack for us."

"Well, what are we waiting for? Let's dive in."

Farrah rummaged for forks and located a cupboard full of plates. She laid them in front of Ginny, who cut the cake. The recipe had called for a coffee cake to be baked inside a cast-iron skillet, which she had found among the mountain of pots and pans that had been left with the home.

The top of the cake was perfectly brown and crisp along the edges. When Ginny cut out a slice, steam burst from the inside, revealing a ribbon of cinnamon winding its way through the delightful snack. The heady fragrance trickled up her nose, and she sighed with delight. There were few things better than a warm cup of coffee and steaming cake to go with it.

At least, she thought so.

"This is heaven," Farrah gushed. "Why haven't you made it before?"

"Well," she admitted, heavyhearted, "Jack never liked any of the recipes from that book. He said they had too much fat and sugar."

"Oh, phooey," Farrah retorted. "He was such a fuddy-duddy. Never wanted to have fun." She took another bite and moaned. "Well, I think it's wonderful, and Jack should've taken the time to appreciate it. *And you.*"

They had already had the Jack discussion, and Ginny didn't want to keep rehashing the details of how shamefully she'd been cast aside like dirty laundry.

"But you've got a new life here, and I love the home," Farrah added, stabbing another bite of coffee cake with her fork. "So. What're you going to do with it?"

"I don't know." She dropped her face into her hands. "Am I crazy, Farrah? For buying it?"

Her friend tipped her head from side to side in thought. "Maybe, but it's the ballsiest thing you've ever done. Face it—you never would've taken such a leap if Jack were still alive."

"Of course not. I would've had all the security I needed."

"And still wouldn't have had a husband you could completely call your own."

Ginny's heart cracked in two. Even if Jack were still alive, she would've been unknowingly sharing him. That was probably why he'd made her be so tight with money, why he'd had to control the finances— so that his secret remained so.

But how much longer would it have remained a secret? If she was really being honest with herself, not much longer. Jack would've eventually had to tell her the truth and they would've divorced. She might've been able to keep her home, though.

"So. What are you going to do with the lighthouse?" Farrah asked again.

Ginny was at a loss. "When I was touring the place, I could just imagine how cute and cozy this room was as a dining room for a restaurant."

"Then open one," Farrah said, elbowing her in the arm.

"But I've never done anything like that. I don't know how to run a business, decide how much to charge."

"Oh, I can help you with all of that. I do have a degree in accounting in case you've forgotten. Not that I've used it in over twenty years," Farrah mused. "But some things you never forget. And if you recall, before I married, I did hold a job in the hospitality industry. We can discuss the day-to-day business details over the phone, and I'll teach you how to make an Excel spreadsheet to keep track of expenditures. You'll need a P and L sheet, or profit and loss." Ginny's head was already swimming. Farrah must've noticed because she hugged her. "But all of that, we can take in baby steps. You'll be fine. Trust me."

"I don't know," Ginny replied after worrying a small groove into her bottom lip with her teeth.

"The real question," Farrah said, seeming to ignore her friend's discomfort, "is what will you serve?"

"I have no clue, and I'm not even convinced that I should open a restaurant."

"I know!" Farrah spotted the faded lemon-colored cover of the cookbook and snatched it from the stainless-steel counter. "You'll make this."

Ginny was completely and utterly confused. "What are you talking about?"

But Farrah was already leafing through the book. "It's perfect. There are starters, soups, salads. Oh, it has a cheese and eggs section. I just love old cookbooks. Lots of casseroles. And the desserts! There's cherries jubilee! How wonderful. Yes, this is a fabulous idea. And there's so much seafood, which is great since you now live at the beach."

She now lived at the beach. What a strange thought. "Wait, Farrah. Slow down."

Farrah closed the hardback book and smiled as if she knew a secret, which Ginny realized that her best friend did. "Okay. You've never owned a restaurant before, and you can't exactly afford to hire staff—wait. Is that true?"

Ginny nodded in shame. "There's no more money. I spent most of it on a lighthouse that doesn't work."

Farrah poked the air with authority. "One problem at a time. Okay, since it'll just be you running this, let me tell you my plan. You don't have to go along with it, but tell me what you think."

She tapped the cookbook, and Ginny knew what her best friend in all the world was thinking. "You want me to use recipes from the book."

"Exactly. You serve one meal a day—lunch. You cook enough for two seatings—an eleven o'clock and a twelve-thirty. You make a salad or soup, entree and dessert each day. But you only cook the one meal. The menu changes daily, and people get what you serve or they don't eat here."

She let that sink in, and started to realize the brilliance of Farrah's plan. Ginny had entertained plenty of times. She'd doubled and even tripled lots of recipes. This would be the exact same. All she would need to do was pick out what three things she would cook for the day, and then she'd double or triple the ingredients. People would get whatever was on the menu for that lunch service, and it would change daily. If people didn't like it, they didn't have to eat there. Plus, working through the cookbook would be a way to honor her grandmother, and she'd be able to do what she loved—create meals and share wonderful food with people.

She pulled Farrah to her and kissed her cheek. "This might be the most brilliant and craziest idea you've ever had."

Farrah grinned widely. Her ash-blonde hair was graying above her ears, and she had fine lines on her forehead, but her youthfulness lay in her love for life. "You will make this work. I just know it. Folks will line up to come taste your creations. Besides, now you can enjoy all the crab you missed out on for years because of Jack. Let me see this book."

She flipped the pages back until she stopped and jabbed the book with her finger. "Right here it is. The best recipe that I know of for a light and delicious crab salad."

"Let me guess—West Indies Salad."

"Exactly! It's light and wonderful. It'll have to be a dish you serve the first week, to honor the beach."

Ginny felt lighter just thinking of this plan. If she could keep the shot of confidence that Farrah had given her, then she might be able to see the restaurant become a success.

But insecurity gnawed at her. Ginny had never endeavored to do anything like this before. Would she succeed at it? Could she do it?

Well, she had the space for it, so she might as well give it a try.

She smiled widely and pulled the cookbook toward her. "Since you're here, let's come up with a few meal plans."

"A few?" Farrah scoffed. "We'll plan an entire month so that you don't have to worry about a thing. And I bet we can meet a local fisherman who will give you fish at a discount if you advertise for them, make sure you boast where the seafood came from."

"Great idea. I love it. But..."

Farrah's brows arched high. "But what? Don't tell me you're hesitating."

"No, not that. I was just wondering, what do we call it?"

"Mm. Well, it's a café inside a lighthouse, so how about the Lighthouse Café?"

She loved it. "It's perfect! Let's get back to menu planning."

They were one week in when Farrah turned to her. "About Reece and Chandler. You've got to call and tell them, the sooner the better."

Ginny knew and it was a conversation that she was dreading. She was about to say as much when her phone rang. She picked it up from the counter and shuddered.

"Well, I suppose there's no time like the present," she told her oldest friend in the world.

"Why's that?"

She flashed the screen toward her. "Because Reece is calling right now."

CHAPTER 7

Chandler

For the last few months Chandler Rigby had felt empty. The emptiness had started before her father's death, and ever since then it had become worse.

It hadn't deepened because her father had influenced her ability to create beautiful jewelry. That wasn't it at all. It was because the grief she felt drained her, and that taxed her skill even more.

Chandler lay in bed staring at the ceiling. She had to get up. She *needed* to get up. She owed Sophie the last piece for the jewelry show, a necklace. It was almost done. All it required was that she rise and finish it.

Her phone rang, and she swiped it from the table. Hudson Wheeler was FaceTiming her.

Even though she felt deflated, Hudson always brought a smile to her eyes.

She pushed the button to answer. "Good morning."

"Good morning, beautiful." His dark brown hair was freshly washed. It was thick, wavy and curled at the collar when it grew an inch too long. His eyes were the color of melted chocolate, and they held a warmth that made Chandler's heart sing.

Hudson reclined in the leather chair that sat in his office. Over his shoulder she spotted the New York City skyline.

"Still asleep?" he asked.

"No. I'm up. Can't you tell?"

"Funny how your workspace looks a lot like your bed."

"Very funny." She sat up. "See? I'm up."

He stared at her a moment, and Chandler felt like Hudson was looking into her soul. She squirmed under the weight of his gaze, hoping he didn't see the desert she felt lived inside of her.

"We still on for dinner tonight after the MOMA?"

"Course we are. What time does the show begin?"

"Four. Earlier than most because John didn't want to be tied down there too late."

"Your successful cousin is so demanding," she teased.

He smiled. "There's something I'd like to talk to you about tonight."

"Is this about a vacation in Paris?" she joked.

Hudson laughed and the corners of his eyes crinkled. "That could happen. After John's opening."

John was his cousin, and his art was being showcased at the MOMA. The opening was tonight. If you asked Chandler, all of Hudson's family was talented. He was a brilliant lawyer; his cousins were either artists or musicians. Plus the Wheelers were wealthy, and his parents heavily contributed to the arts.

They were all fabulously successful, and she couldn't even get out of bed.

"But yes, the MOMA and then dinner," he said. "If you're up for it."

Then he gave her *that look*. A look with sympathy written all over it. Chandler knew that she wasn't as fun and gleeful as she had been when they first met a year ago. She couldn't explain why. But before her father ever died, something inside of her was tightening. She felt like she was smothering, and after he passed, she felt like something inside of her broke.

But Chandler had never admitted that to anybody, especially not to someone as successful and handsome as Hudson, who came from a long line of successful and handsome stock.

"I'll see you then," she promised.

"I love you, beautiful."

She smiled. "I love you, too."

They hung up and she got to work.

* * *

By lunchtime the piece was done. It was rectangular garnet with gold wire wrapped around the stone. A single diamond was set into the gold frame on the top left. The style reflected her quintessential fashion—angular and modern.

She took inspiration from her surroundings, from New York City itself. She had moved to the city with a degree in jewelry design and a dream to create pieces that people wanted to wear. And she had done it.

Within her first year she had met Sophie Granger, who owned the most prestigious gallery in SoHo and who, every year, made it a point to showcase jewelry so that the rich women of the Upper East and West Sides, as well as those in Connecticut, could come and buy one-of-a-kind pieces. Ever since that first year Chandler had been invited back annually to showcase her work.

Now she admired the brown garnet and sighed. It was beautiful. The work was gorgeous, but Chandler's heart wasn't in it.

In fact, she had an entire box of carefully wrapped jewelry that was ready to be delivered to Sophie's, and she hated all of it.

Yet she couldn't put her finger on exactly what was wrong. The pieces simply felt uninspired, dull, unoriginal, like they were reruns of work she'd previously created.

But even though she felt that way, this was all she had, and Sophie's big show always made her so much money that Chandler didn't have to worry about cash for the rest of the year.

She swallowed the knot in her throat as she cleaned the stone with alcohol, and then wrapped it in velvet and placed it with the other pieces, ready to deliver them to Sophie.

* * *

It was a short cab ride from her studio apartment in Greenwich village to SoHo. Sophie spotted her as soon as she entered the door and approached, arms wide.

"Darling, so good to see you. What do you have for me?"

Sophie was tall and dressed in high fashion—bright colors, high heels, thick-rimmed glasses, hair perfectly coiffed. Chandler didn't bother to look down at her own muted colors. Her closet was full of soft grays, light creams and black. Today she wore a heather-gray sweater and matching slacks.

She brushed aside a strand of white-blonde hair that fell into her eyes and placed the box in Sophie's arms. "These are my pieces for the show."

The gallery owner's jaw dropped with surprise. "I can't wait to see them. Shall we?"

"Sure." Her stomach knotted. She did not want to be present when Sophie scoured through her jewelry, but there was no delivering and running. She would stay and cross her fingers that the pieces were up to snuff. "I've got time."

The gallery owner unwrapped the very pendant that had just been created.

She frowned.

A line formed between her brows.

She pursed her lips and gave a slight shake of her head, and then Sophie rewrapped the piece and placed it in the box. "I'll just look at those later." She gave Chandler an air-kiss on each cheek. "I'll see you tonight at the MOMA, right?"

"Of course."

Sophie checked her watched and tsked in impatience. "Darling I would love to chat, but I'm terribly busy. See you then, okay?"

As Chandler stepped out of the gallery, she couldn't ignore the stone in the pit of her stomach. Sophie hadn't said as much, but it was obvious —she'd hated the garnet pendant.

Her biggest fear was blossoming inside of her. It wasn't simply in her mind that she had lost her muse. It was real. Chandler's artistry was gone.

She didn't know what to do.

CHAPTER 8

Ginny

"You bought a lighthouse?" Reece screeched.

Ginny had managed to find the courage to reveal to Reece *some* of what had happened to her, but not all of it. How could she tell her daughter over the phone what Jack had done? It didn't seem fair.

Though she half hoped that Reece would let things drop, her youngest, the more dramatic of her two daughters, did not.

"I'm coming down to see you. Something isn't right," Reece said.

"There's not much room." She did not offer that there was a second bedroom with two twin beds in it. Reece was on a need-to-know basis.

"I'll sleep on the couch."

"There isn't a couch," Ginny told her.

Which was entirely true. The living room was a restaurant dining room.

"Then I'll make a pallet on the floor. You need me, Mama. You can't be alone right now."

"Your Aunt Farrah's here."

"Farrah's there?" The hurt in Reece's voice made Ginny grimace. She really should've called her daughter earlier and told her something, *anything*. She hated that Reece discovered she'd been kicked out of her home by knocking on the front door of her house. Correction, her *previous* house. "Farrah's there?" her daughter repeated.

"Don't worry about me, honey. Everything's fine. You just keep on with your studies."

"Tell me everything about the lighthouse."

And so she did. By the time they hung up, Reece seemed satisfied that everything was okay. At least, that's how it seemed to Ginny.

Farrah stayed several more hours, long enough for the two women to come up with a solid menu that could be planned out for the next month. Then she left, and Ginny found herself very much alone with a lengthy to-do list stretched out before her on a sheet of paper.

She set about planning.

Her next chores were to get her business license and hire vendors. Perhaps a fresh coat of paint on the dining room walls would be a help, too. It certainly couldn't hurt, and it was something that Ginny could do all by herself.

It was an easy task, the easiest of them all, and the one with the least amount of risk. Oh, what was she thinking? She hadn't done anything so daring in her entire life. Jack had always been the risk-taker, not her.

Her greatest fear was falling flat on her face, because she had to accept it; she didn't possess any skills. She simply didn't think that she could make a successful go at a business without Jack behind her.

But even if Jack were still alive (and he hadn't had a mistress and second family), he would've just chuckled if she'd wanted to start a business. In fact, at one point she had suggested getting her real estate license to bring in extra money.

They'd been eating dinner at the time, and Jack had placed his cutting knife on the table and looked at her solemnly. "Do I not make enough money for you?"

"Of course, you do," she said, waving her hand in an attempt to make light of her suggestion. "I just thought a little extra cash couldn't hurt."

It could also mean that her monthly budget would have a little more cushion.

His eyes narrowed. "I can't have my wife running around showing properties. What would my clients think? That I'm not making the money that they think I am? It would embarrass me. You don't want to embarrass me, do you?"

Ginny certainly hadn't been looking to embarrass Jack. "Of course I don't want that for you." She smiled and lifted her fork. "How's your steak?"

And that had been the end of the conversation.

By the time she had made her list of chores that needed to get done and called a few vendors to inquire about setting up an account, it was late.

The sun was beginning to set, and she thought a walk on the beach might do her some good. After all, in the two days that she had been in Sugar Cove, Ginny hadn't had a chance to see the sights in the small town.

She pulled on a pair of sandals and headed down the sandy dune that was her backyard. The lighthouse was positioned right on the beach. Houses flanked both sides and were sprinkled across the street as well. A little ways down were several shops and a restaurant.

School was back in session by September, so the family crowds were long gone from Sugar Cove. But several sunbathers were scattered atop the sugary sands.

The sand itself was warm under her feet. She walked to the water, just before the waves crashed onto the surf. A few crabs crawled sideways into holes, and she spotted bubbles atop the wet sand from clams blowing water from their valves.

As Ginny walked, the water rolled in and kissed her toes. It was soft until it wasn't. Something hard brushed against the outside of her foot. She glanced down and spotted a seashell.

Being used to seeing mostly cracked or shell shards, Ginny was surprised that when she retrieved this particular treasure from the ocean, it was completely intact.

"Got yourself a Scotch bonnet," came a husky masculine voice.

She glanced up quickly. The sea breeze tossed long brown strands of hair into her face before she could pull the tangled pieces away to see who was talking to her.

When she realized who it was, Ginny wished that she could cover her face back up with her hair. "Oh, hello."

"How's the lighthouse?" he asked.

He asked it so casually, as if he hadn't been the person who had basically coaxed her into entering the auction.

"I could've gotten it a lot cheaper if you hadn't bid against me. Not a nice game to play."

"Who said I was playing a game?"

The brazen honesty in his tone made a pit open in her stomach. His words pierced her with so much honesty that Ginny looked away.

"Well"—she kicked a cracked seashell, sending it flipping over just once before it became suctioned to the wet sand—"why else would you have bid against me if it wasn't a game?"

He extended one long arm, flicking his fingers, gesturing for the seashell in her palm. She gave it to him, and he turned it over.

"For your information, I wanted to buy the lighthouse, but I was outbid by a city woman."

She threw her head back and laughed at that. "We city women have bite."

"But the snail that used to live inside this shell didn't."

"Oh?" She peered closer as he swept his fingers over the milky lip of the shell. The back was patterned with dark squares of tan inside a grid made of lighter tan. "A snail lived inside?"

"Yep, and you're lucky that a hermit crab hasn't snatched the shell for itself."

She quirked a brow. "Maybe one has."

He inspected it closer, and that was when Ginny got a good long look at him. He was midfifties maybe, with mostly dark hair that was graying at the temples. His skin was tan, suggesting he spent time in the sun, and his arms and legs were muscular, his stomach flat.

He exercised a lot more than most men his age who were fighting off the middle-age spread.

"If you'd wanted the lighthouse so badly," she asked, "why'd you suggest I bid on it?"

He shrugged before glancing from the shell to peer into her eyes. His bright blue eyes sparked with intelligence.

"Because I sensed that somehow, you might need the place, too."

Her throat closed. Ginny didn't know what or even how to express what she felt, because she hadn't experienced a stirring like that for a long, long time.

She pushed her feelings aside and took a step back. "Well, then."

It wasn't a brilliant comeback, but she couldn't think of anything else to say.

He tried to hand the seashell back to her, but Ginny tossed out, "Keep it. I think you need it, too."

"What's your name?"

She considered not telling him just for the fun of it but decided it was best not to play games. "Virginia Rigby, but everyone calls me Ginny."

"Well, Ginny, my name's Aiden."

She started to walk backward toward the lighthouse. "You got a last name?"

"Everyone calls me Aiden."

With that, Aiden slipped the seashell into his pocket before giving her one last look and walking away.

CHAPTER 9

Chandler

The Metropolitan Museum of Art was bustling with people. Waiters and waitresses balanced on their fingertips silver trays laden with champagne flutes. They scurried from guest to guest offering refreshments. Other trays filled with hors d'oeuvres were being passed through the crowd as well. But all of it was just a buzzing noise in the back of Chandler's head.

"Hey, you in there?" Hudson lightly touched her elbow. "Are you awake?"

She blinked and smiled. "Of course. I'm good."

"Come on, let's go say hello to John."

They found John surrounded by Hudson's family. Chandler smiled and nodded. Hudson's mother, Evelyn, gave her a light kiss on the cheek.

"Maybe one day your pieces will be in here," she said encouragingly.

The knot in her stomach had only gotten bigger since she'd left the art gallery earlier that day. It threatened to take over her throat and stem her ability to speak.

"Yes, maybe," she replied, trying to sound enthusiastic even though she was withering on the inside.

Hudson sidled up beside his mother. "Mind if I steal Chandler for a moment?"

Evelyn took a step back. "Of course not." She was wearing a tasteful black dress and pear-drop earrings encrusted with diamonds that must've cost a fortune. "Enjoy the show, dear."

Chandler smiled. "I will."

"Let's walk." Hudson steered her gently toward the show, and Chandler's jaw dropped at the paintings.

The colors were bold, the angles inspired. Even John's self-portrait had energy and life.

"So," Hudson said, "penny for your thoughts?"

"The pieces are amazing."

"Not that. What's bothering you?"

"Nothing's bothering me." She shrugged. "I'm fine."

He stopped at the end of a hall and turned to face her, his mouth dipping into a frown, his dimples peeking out from his cheeks. "Chandler Rigby, I've known you long enough to realize when you're lying."

"It's nothing."

"Hmm." His eyes narrowed slightly, suggesting he didn't believe her. "Have I ever told you what I thought when we first met?"

"No." Her gaze drifted around the room. "That you liked art?"

"No," he said flatly. "I realized that—"

"Oh, there's Sophie." The gallery owner spotted her and smiled, causing the knot in Chandler's stomach to slowly unfurl. Maybe her pieces weren't as uninspired as she thought. Perhaps Sophie had liked them after all. She whipped away from Hudson and said over her shoulder, "I'll be right back."

She skirted as quickly as she dared without looking like an art thief toward Sophie.

"Darling, we meet again," Sophie cooed.

Chandler had little interest in chit-chat but forced herself to be polite. "Yes, so glad. I'm hoping you liked the jewelry?"

"Well, darling, here's the thing. As much as I hate to say it, I don't think I've got a spot for you this year in the show."

The world fell out from under her feet. "What?"

Sophie sighed. "This isn't something I want to have to tell you, you should know that. We've been friends a long time, and so I must be honest with you, no matter how brutal. Chandler, your art simply isn't as inspired as it has been in the past. The pieces are dull, boring. You've lost something. Look, I know that your father's death has been hard. Maybe you need some time off."

Her fingers and toes were numb. "Time off?"

She couldn't take time off. She needed money. She had to live. New York was outrageously expensive.

"Take some time," Sophie was saying, but Chandler was barely listening. "Get your muse back. Maybe get married. Evelyn says that Hudson's going to ask."

"What?" How would getting married help anything?

"Just get inspired, darling," Sophie told her. "Oh, I must go. Chat soon."

Sophie walked away, leaving her very much alone in the bustling room full of art lovers. She slowly lifted her gaze and spotted Hudson. Their gazes locked and he started to make his way over.

In that moment, several thoughts rushed through her mind. The first, it was confirmed—she had lost her muse. The second, she couldn't give herself to anyone until she had figured out what was wrong inside of her. And third, she wasn't nearly good enough for Hudson's family, not now that she was a second-rate jewelry artist without a home.

As Hudson approached, her phone rang. Desperate for any excuse not to have to tell him what had just happened, she slid it from her clutch and was surprised to see Reece's name on the screen.

Chandler and her sister barely spoke. They were only three years apart, but they simply didn't *get* one another. They didn't call each other to chat about their days. They barely chatted at holidays.

So why was Reece calling now? Curiosity piqued inside her; plus she still needed a distraction. "Hello?"

Reece didn't even bother with salutations. "There's something going on with Mama."

She listened as she explained something about their mother no longer living in Buckhead. It all sounded very confusing, and what it mostly sounded like was that Chandler now had an excuse to not have to hear what it was Hudson was going to ask her at dinner later that night.

He stood beside her, eyebrows knitted in worry, as she listened. When Chandler hung up, he said, "Is everything okay?"

She shook her head. "No, it's not. My mama needs me, and I need to leave. Now."

44

CHAPTER 10

Ginny

Whe had she been thinking when she threw Aiden's own words back at him, suggesting he needed the seashell? And then he took it?

Had she been flirting with him? Had *he* been flirting with *her?*

Goodness, the way he looked at her in that last moment right before he walked away had sent a ripple through her spine. No man had looked at her that way in...years.

Goodness knew that Jack hadn't. Their sex life had been nonexistent for months up until he died. Now that she had clarity on the situation, she realized his inattentiveness was more than likely due to his mistress and second family.

And of course, his planning to give her house to That Woman.

Anger suddenly burned in her gut like acid. Somehow her grief from the past several days had suddenly vanished and in its place was white-hot rage. If Jack hadn't been dead and was standing right in front of her, Ginny would have let him have it.

She thought of how much she had scrimped and saved even though Jack was bringing home millions. For years she had been a sucker, used by the man who was supposed to have loved her.

Love. *What a crock.*

She was back in the lighthouse now and was beelining directly toward the kitchen freezer to claim the gallon of ice cream that she'd bought, when a knock came from her front door.

Who could it be? She didn't know anyone in town.

To her surprise, when she opened the door, she found not one of her daughters but both of them.

Reece hugged her. "Mama, thank goodness that you're alive. I was so worried."

"How did y'all get here so fast?" she asked, baffled.

Reece dropped her hands and wheeled her suitcase into the house. She rested it against a wall and slung her purse over her shoulder. "I drove fast as I could without getting a ticket, and Chandler caught the first flight out."

Ginny stared at her in shock. "I told you on the phone that I was fine. You didn't have to come."

"Not good enough for our Reece's cup." Chandler wheeled a much smaller, more compact bag into the front room. "Oh, this is nice. I love it. The color is so sunny."

She glared at her sister. "Can we please not discuss how nice the new place is? What's going on with the old place? Why is that woman living in it?"

Chandler folded her arms. "You promised, Reece."

All the commotion was making Ginny's head spin. "Promised what?"

Reece dropped her head back and stared at the ceiling. "I promised to give it at least five minutes before giving you the third degree."

"Ten. You promised ten." Chandler hugged and kissed her mother. "How're you?"

Ginny stared into the bright brown eyes of her oldest. Chandler was always so lovely—tall and thin, beautiful without having to work at it. She could have any man that she wanted, but all Chandler wanted was Hudson Wheeler, the lawyer. Ginny wasn't complaining. She'd met him twice. He seemed kind, attentive. The sort of man who would make her daughter happy.

"Mama?" Chandler took her by the hand and gently shook it. "You in there?"

"Yes." Ginny, realizing that there was no getting rid of her unexpected company (not that she wanted to, for she loved her girls) said, "I was just about to have some ice cream. Would y'all like some?"

"What flavor?" Reece, the picky eater asked.

"Rocky road."

"I'm in. Chandler?"

She waved it away. "No thanks. I'm good."

She made two bowls of ice cream and gave the girls a tour of the lighthouse as Reece loudly ate. Her spoon scraped the side of the bowl every few seconds. That occurred between her sharp comments about the home.

"You can't actually want to live here...it's cool that it has a spiral staircase...don't fall from up there...where's the closet?...you can't be serious about this place."

Ginny, for what it was worth, spent the tour trying to decide whether she should tell the girls the truth about what had happened. She'd managed to dodge Reece's pushy questions over the phone, but she wouldn't be able to keep anything a secret for much longer.

Or would she?

When all three women were on Ginny's bed, she said, "You're wondering what happened. Why the sudden move."

"Heck yes, we are," Reece said.

"Why were you visiting me in the first place? Your semester isn't over yet," she inquired.

Her youngest squirmed atop the bed and smoothed her hands down her jeans. "I just wanted to visit you. See how you're doing. My professors all know this is a stressful time."

The way her daughter skirted her gaze made Ginny think there was more going on than her daughter simply wanting to ambush her with a surprise visit.

She quickly changed the topic. "But why did you move so suddenly without calling us?"

"It *is* a mystery, Mama," Chandler added in her easygoing way.

Both of her girls had picked perfect professions for their temperaments. Chandler was always so laid back and dreamy, so artistry was in her blood from birth. Reece had always been much more Type A—even when she was a little girl, when all her toys had to be put in the correct place. Since doctors had to pay sharp attention to detail, the medical profession had seemed a great choice for her.

"Mama," Reece prodded her. "Why are you here?"

It was a strange sensation to be grilled by her own daughter. Ginny decided she didn't care one lick for the feeling. "Well," she said slowly, making her decision about what to say right then and there, "I wanted a change."

It wasn't a lie, just not the complete truth.

"But why? Our home was perfect," Reece demanded.

"Is there something that we should be worried about?" Chandler's eyes filled with concern. "Are you okay?"

She squeezed her daughter's hand. "Yes, I'm fine. But after the will reading"—her heart tightened just thinking about it—"I knew that I couldn't stay there, in that house. So, I packed some things and left."

"But that woman who answered the door said you had to leave quickly. Who is she? Is she renting it?"

Uh-oh. Ginny was quickly being sucked into the quicksand of her lies. "No, she bought it. I'd talked to Dane about selling it earlier, before..."

Hopefully they didn't ask before what. She didn't have a good answer for that.

"But what about my bedroom and all my stuff? That woman wouldn't let me in," Reece complained.

Her heart constricted. In her hurry, she hadn't given a thought about her daughter. Reece still had a perfectly intact bedroom that hadn't been completely cleaned out when she'd moved for medical school. After all, she only slept in the house on holidays. It wasn't as if Reece's most precious possessions were in that room. Her real life was in New Orleans.

Still, guilt washed over Ginny. She should've fought harder to stay at least one day so that she could've worked through the madness.

Anger built up like two fists pushing against her chest cavity trying to break free. This was all Jack's fault. She hoped, wherever he was, that he was suffering.

All she could say to ease Reece's worry was, "We'll get your things, honey. Don't worry about that. Whatever you want."

Surely That Woman would allow Reece to come inside and take whatever she needed. Hopefully Savannah had some sort of heart.

Chandler flashed her mother a sincere smile. "I was surprised that you didn't call us, but I do like it here. I love the salty air and think this place will be good for you."

From the frown creasing Reece's face, she suspected that her youngest daughter's feelings were the exact opposite.

"Wonderful." Ginny settled her bowl, clacking spoon and all, on the nightstand. "Well, I didn't mean to scare you, and tomorrow y'all can get back to your lives. I don't want to impose. I've a lot of work to do here."

The frown became a crater. "What sort of work?"

"I'm opening a restaurant."

And where she expected Reece to be angry, the exact opposite happened. For the first time, she cracked a smile. "That's amazing. You are? Can I help?"

It was Ginny's turn to be dumbfounded. "Help? You've got medical school. You need to return to Tulane."

Reece lifted her arms and let them fall limply to the bed. "My professors are allowing me some time off." When Ginny frowned, she added, "They already told me that I can make up some classes in summer school."

Well, if she remained committed to her goals, taking a few weeks off couldn't hurt anything. "If there was one thing your father wanted, it was to see you become a doctor."

"I know. I'm going to make him proud. But"—she shook Ginny gently—"you're opening a restaurant. What kind of food?"

She laughed as she told them Farrah's brilliant idea to bake and fry her way through the cookbook that she'd inherited from her grandmother.

"I've always loved that book," her daughter gushed. "Grandma and I would make chocolate cookies from it. I always wondered why you never cooked out of it more."

Ginny bit back some nasty words about her dead husband. "Better late than never, right? I'm going to cook from it now."

"Then I'll help however I can," she announced. "It'll be good for us to do this. What about you, Chandler?"

She nibbled her finger. Ginny wanted to let her off the hook. "If you need to return to New York, go ahead. Don't you have a show coming up?"

Chandler winced as if suffering from a flash of pain. But then Ginny's oldest quickly smiled. "Um. Yes. The show is coming up soon. I'll need to get back to it. But I'm sure it would be okay if I stayed a few days, help with whatever you need to get the business up and running."

Ginny hugged her daughters to her chest. The girls seemed as happy as they could be, given the magnitude of the loss that they had all recently suffered. But even so, she couldn't help but notice that both of them seemed distracted. Perhaps it was all in her head. After all, they'd been worried about her and had dropped everything to track her down. Yes, that was probably it. It was their worrying that her mother's intuition had picked up on.

But she couldn't stop herself from thinking there was more to this visit. There was something the girls weren't telling her.

But what could it be?

CHAPTER 11

Reece

Reece was elated. Cooking was something she loved, and she rarely had any time for with her busy class and study schedule. Since she didn't want to worry her mother about Tulane (as her mother was clearly suffering from a mental breakdown—why else would she have sold the house without telling them?), she would wait to tell the truth about her semester until a later date.

"Have you been to the top of the lighthouse?" Reece asked, standing at the foot of the stairwell beside her mother, who wore a light silk robe over her pajamas. She shivered and shook her head.

"No, no. Small spaces aren't my thing."

Reece's jaw fell. "You mean, you bought the lighthouse without ever going up it?"

She ran a hand over her weary face. "Some things you don't have to see to know that you want."

Reece understood that. Her heart became encased in a tomb of nervousness when she thought about school. But when her mind floated to cooking for the new café, all that tension loosened and she felt free.

Her arms tightened around a swath of blankets and pillows. "I'm going to sleep up there. If it's all right, that is."

Her mother gestured up the stairs. "Be my guest. My home is your home. But you'll want a light."

She turned her body so that her mother could spy her crossbody purse. "Got one right here. My phone."

"Oh, right." Her mother rubbed the back of her neck. "Sometimes I forget about all the modern conveniences." She paused. "Are you sure you don't want to sleep in the extra bedroom with your sister?"

There went that tightness again. When Reece had entered the bedroom earlier, Chandler was sitting on the bed, scrolling through her phone. She hadn't even looked up to greet her.

"Want to sleep upstairs, in the tower?" Reece had asked, enthusiasm bouncing around in her body. They were at the beach! Living in a lighthouse! How cool was that?

"No thanks. I'm fine down here."

Chandler seemed distracted, so Reece asked, "Everything okay?"

"Everything's fine." The corners of her mouth wrinkled into a frown. "I'm just tired. It's been a long day."

Reece knew her sister was lying, but she didn't push. You couldn't cross a chasm in a day, and the valley that had existed between them their whole lives wasn't going to be filled and crossable in one night.

"Okay, then," was all she had said as she pulled blankets and pillows from the bed. They were freshly washed and Reece was grateful.

Her mother gave her a hug good night, and Reece carried the blankets and pillows up the spiral staircase. Her thighs ached as she counted the steps. It was when she reached one hundred and eight that she was at the top. She shoved her load through the small hole and hoisted herself into the tower. There, she rose and peered out at the town below.

The lights from the interior of beach houses dotted the shoreline. Even though it was dark, she spotted waves crashing against the surf. Her heart ballooned.

This was where she was supposed to be.

She pulled the phone from her purse and made the pallet. Then she pulled her hair from the ponytail she usually always kept in it because the style was easy and quick to do, a necessity when you were running late for class.

Reece sank onto the pile of blankets and fell asleep to the sound of crashing waves.

When she awoke, a dark sky just beginning to brighten greeted her. She felt around until she found her cell phone. She turned on the light and spotted her purse. She lifted it and the pen fell out. The pen seemed to stare at her accusingly.

You're letting me down, it seemed to whisper.

She stuffed it back inside the purse and got up, stretching the kinks from her body. It had been cool to sleep in the tower for one night, but unless she got a mattress up there, she doubted that her body could survive many more nights on the hard floor.

She bounded down the stairs and eyed her reflection in a hanging mirror as she passed it by.

Limp brown hair hung to her shoulders. Her brows were thick and framed her face well, but her hair could use a new style. To her own eyes, Reece was plain and boring.

She sighed and shoved away her insecurities. She might not be a beauty, but Reece had other talents and she planned to use them here, in the lighthouse.

As the first one to rise, she made a pot of coffee. While she waited for the coffee to brew, she spotted the open cookbook on the counter and started reading through it.

The joyous glee that filled her was nearly embarrassing. All her life Reece had loved to cook, but when it came time to deciding what to do with her life, *medicine it was,* her father had declared. He'd had one child who was an artist, and he wanted the other to be a professional.

She scoured over the casseroles and then flipped to the salads to try to think up pairings that would make a fantastic meal.

The door opened as the coffee finished dripping and Chandler entered.

She wore black leggings and a loose-fitting black top over a sports bra. Her hair was swept back, and her cheeks were ruddy from exercise. Chandler could've been dipped in mud, and she still would've looked beautiful. Reece envied how effortless it was for her sister to look fabulous.

Reece had to work at it. She never left the house without mascara applied and lip gloss coating her mouth. Her eyelashes were nonexistent unless she made them stand out, and her features were pretty but simple. She didn't possess the same natural glamour that Chandler did.

"You're already up?" Reece asked, surprised. She knew that Chandler worked hard, but she was an artist. They weren't exactly known for rising and shining.

"I wanted to see the beach at sunrise. There's something beautiful about it, don't you think?"

"I do think so." Reece poured herself a cup of coffee and held it with both hands, savoring the imprints of warmth it left on her skin. Chandler glanced in the direction of the bedroom, and she added, "Mama's asleep. I already checked."

"Think she's got any tea?"

"Don't know. Didn't look."

Chandler searched through the cupboards. "None. Coffee it is, I guess." She poured a cup and pulled up a stool beside Reece. "What're you doing?"

"Making up menus."

"For what?"

"For the restaurant."

"Of course." Chandler pulled the book to her. "That'll help Mama out when you return to school."

Reece nodded but didn't say anything.

"Why aren't you answering?"

"I thought I did."

She glanced up from the book and studied her sister. Ever since they were little, when Chandler focused her laser attention on Reece, she always felt like her sister was picking her apart from the inside out.

"Stop," she said.

"Stop what?"

"Doing whatever it is that you're doing."

"I'm not doing anything," Chandler said softly.

"You're judging me." Reece stretched the neck of her T-shirt over her nose. "Stop judging me. You always do."

Her mouth pressed into a frowny bow. "I don't always judge you." Reece cleared her throat, and her sister rolled her eyes. "Besides, how can I judge you if there's nothing to judge?" When she didn't answer, Chandler's eyes popped wide. "Reece, what's going on?"

"Nothing."

Her voice dropped to a fierce whisper. "There is too something going on. What is it?"

"I just...might not go back to school this semester."

"You're failing," she said flatly.

"No, I'm not." She backed away, needing to put distance between them. Her sister would never understand because her life hadn't been plotted out for her. "Look, I just need a break. It's too much with Dad dying. I can't focus. I can't study. I'm not doing anyone any good there. It's better if I just take a break and regroup. Return in the summer."

Chandler watched her for a long time before saying, "You've got to tell Mama. She's expecting you to finish and become a doctor like you always planned."

For a long time Reece believed that she wanted to be a doctor. It wasn't until her father passed that she felt all the wind in her sails for medicine die down. With him gone, the goal no longer seemed important. Instead it felt like thigh-high mud she was slogging through.

"I'm going to finish," Reece replied more defensively than she'd intended. Feeling frustrated, she smoothed her hands down her hair to calm herself.

But even as she insisted that she would finish medical school, her chest constricted. The thought of graduating and then moving on to her residency made her stomach flip in fear. It felt like her world was closing in, that she didn't have room to breathe because she was fulfilling someone else's wish for her life.

Chandler studied Reece for a moment more and nodded, seeming satisfied with her answer. "I just want to make sure you're happy."

Happy? When did Chandler care about her happiness?

"I'm happy," she lied. "Of course I am. I'm doing what I always intended to do."

But what if medical school wasn't what she was *supposed* to do? What if there was another route for her to take? One that would actually make her happy? Was it worth it to travel that path and, by doing so, let down her family?

Or would it just be better for Reece to do what she'd always done, grin and bear it?

"But anyway, I'm going to stay," she said. "At least until the restaurant opens. Mama could use our help, don't you think?"

She nodded absently. "Yeah, she could."

Now Reece felt the need to press her sister. "Will you help open the café?"

"I don't know. I've got so much going on at home."

Reece always thought the best way to guilt someone was to say nothing, so she just nodded. "I get it."

"I would stay," she said, her hand to her neck. Her sister always did that when she was uncomfortable. "It's just..."

The art show. That was what she was worried about. Reece stared into her coffee. "Mama will understand, whatever you do."

But *she* wouldn't. Their mother might accept Chandler abandoning them after discovering she'd bought a *lighthouse* (of all things) and was opening a café, but Reece would not.

Their family had shrunk by one, which meant the three of them needed to stick together. They were all they had.

As Chandler sipped her coffee, Reece couldn't help but wonder how the art show could be more important than their family.

"You do what you want," she said. "I know your art is important to your livelihood."

"It is." Chandler ran her finger over the rim of the glass. "I used to find such beauty in things that were man-made, like this cup. The rim is a simple gorgeous circle. Buildings are the same way with their sharp edges. I took so much enjoyment from simply looking at the shapes and using them to fill up my artistic well. But lately..."

Reece searched her sister. "Lately what?"

She sighed and dropped her perfectly unlined forehead onto the counter. "Lately I haven't been feeling it, any of it. I've barely admitted this to myself, so I'm surprised that I'm telling it to you."

"Thanks," Reece said sarcastically.

"Sorry, but you know. We don't talk much. But anyway, I just don't feel my art anymore." She paused, seeming to search for the right word. "And I think that I might want to stop creating. For good."

CHAPTER 12
Chandler

R ight after she told Reece her struggles, Chandler took her coffee cup outside and returned to the beach. The knot that formed in her chest felt like a fist pushing on her heart.

Admitting she'd lost her muse to herself was one thing. Admitting it to her sister, a person she barely spoke to, was another.

For so long her art had been part of what made her heart beat, and now Chandler didn't know what would fill that space anymore, what would inspire her, keep her going.

She glanced up, not wanting to think about it.

The sun had broken away from the horizon a while ago, and the beach was awash with its golden hues. Seagulls floated on the air currents before her. She admired the lines of their wings as they tipped and rose above the ocean.

A flock of pelicans floated on the water. They weren't a handsome bird, but their silhouette demanded they be paid attention to with their cone-like beaks and rounded bodies.

It was a different world here than what she had wrapped herself in the past few years. For so long she'd thought the city held everything that she wanted. But out here, with the sand filling the space between her toes and with skyline as far as she could see, Chandler felt herself open.

Inside the pocket built into her leggings, her phone rang. She fished it out and saw Hudson's name flash. She answered and his beautifully handsome face filled the screen.

"Good morning, beautiful," he said in his velvety voice that made her heart constrict.

She cringed at how she'd abandoned him the night before. She'd apologized for having to leave so suddenly. But Hudson, being the gentleman that he was, didn't complain once as he rode with Chandler to her apartment and helped her pack. Then he wouldn't hear of her waiting for a commercial flight, so he pulled some strings and managed to get her on a client's private jet.

Yes, dating him had its perks.

"Good morning," she replied. "I hope your family isn't totally disappointed that I left early."

He shook his head. "Not at all." He was sitting up in his bed. The dark brown headboard was a perfect backdrop. Hudson wore a T-shirt that stretched over his chest. This was gorgeous Saturday morning Hudson—her favorite look. Her heart ached to be beside him, curled up with a cup of coffee and reading the paper.

"Is your mom okay?" he asked.

"She's fine. Bought a lighthouse and is going to turn it into a café."

He laughed. "You're kidding."

"Nope. And I'm going to help."

His smile faded, but he quickly recovered by clearing his throat. "But you'll be back in time for Sophie's show, right?"

She should tell him now. She should tell him the truth. But all that came out was, "I hope so. Mama's got a challenge ahead of her, and I'd like to help."

He adjusted his position and tucked a hand beneath his head. "Does she seem okay? I mean, it's not every day someone moves and buys a lighthouse."

"Honestly"—Chandler thought back to their bedtime discussion over ice cream—"she seems *okay*. But I feel like there's more going on that she isn't saying. She needs me."

"I need you, too."

"Oh, you don't need me. You've got so much to keep you busy."

"I like having you keep me busy."

Heat flared on her cheeks, and Chandler shook her head. "Stop it. But seriously, I'm going to stay for at least a week."

"Okay, but don't stay too long. You've got a life here, remember?"

Her stomach became a whirlwind of butterflies at his words. She didn't understand the building tension and needed a distraction.

She blew him an air-kiss that he caught. "I know that I've got a life there. Don't worry. I won't abandon New York. There's no way that I could give up the city for the beach."

There was no way. New York was where life, *her life,* was.

He sighed heavily. "Goodbye, beautiful. Saturday won't be the same without you."

"Bye, Hudson."

Chandler hung up and exhaled a gusty breath. She dropped the phone to her side and glanced out at the horizon.

She needed a break, she realized. It wouldn't kill her to stay a few days, help her mother open the restaurant. In fact, it might feel good to dig her hands into some work, bus tables, take orders, or whatever it was that she could do.

Sophie's show would go on without her. As much as Chandler was devastated that she wouldn't be a part of it, she knew she needed this time to herself to figure things out.

As she stared out into the ocean, a triangle cut across the water. Even seeing a shark far out from the beach brought calm to her. She inhaled deeply and exhaled.

A light snapping on at the lighthouse caught her attention. Her mama was up. Chandler took one last look at the water crashing onto the shore and thought she should go inside to see what she could do to help her mother get the lighthouse ready to become a restaurant.

CHAPTER 13

Reece

When she scrolled through her emails a few days after she
arrived, the first one that grabbed her attention was from
Dr. Creigs at Tulane.

Reece,
   *Your absence from class has resulted in a grade of zero for your last
exam. Please see me so that we can discuss.*
   Dr. Creigs

That was him—short and to the point. She stared at the email and felt
the weight of her decision to leave school like a barbell pushing down on
her shoulders.

Though she'd told her mother and sister that the administration at
Tulane was fine with her absence, Reece had failed to actually *tell* the
administration that she would be absent.

She felt as helpless as when she was a child after having been put to
bed for the night. She always watched the dark corner of her room, the
one that held her closet, carefully, convinced a monster would sneak out
in the dark and eat her.

Her parents always told her there were no monsters, and she hadn't known they were there at all until Chandler told her they were inside, just waiting to suck her brains out while she slept.

Needless to say, that had put a damper on Reece's relationship with her sister, one that had lasted up until, well, now, and continued to do so.

Maybe getting the Lighthouse Café up and running would be good for them. Maybe they would become close, the way sisters were supposed to be.

She stared at the email and sighed. How could she tell her mother that Tulane wasn't her dream? That just thinking of returning to school made her stomach sour?

She couldn't. Her mama had been through too much. Reece had to email her professor back. She had to email the dean of the medical school and ask for her semester to be put on hold. She had to do all those things.

But instead of doing that, Reece decided to scour the beach for shells. She slipped on a pair of canvas shoes and headed out. The sun was high in the sky, and the salty breeze swept her hair off her neck and whipped it onto her face. Reece pulled it into a ponytail and proceeded to search for washed-up shells.

She found a few, and after half an hour her mouth was dry from thirst, so she headed across the street to the gas station.

"Welcome," came a chipper voice.

Her gaze drifted through the store until she located the owner of the voice, a redhead about her age with gorgeous, lush hair, and makeup artfully and delicately applied.

"Hey," Reece said.

The young woman squinted at her. "You've been staying at the light-house, right?"

Her stomach tightened. Was she being spied on?

The woman just laughed. "Sorry, didn't mean to make you feel para-noid. Sugar Cove is a small town. I've driven by when you've been coming out."

She instantly relaxed. "Yeah, I am living there. My mom bought it."

"I met her. She came in the morning of the auction. So. Are you moving in?"

Reece laughed as she made her way to the wall of bottled drinks and grabbed a water. "I'm not moving in permanently. My mama's turning the place into a café, and I'm helping her out. Me and my sister, that is."

The woman's eyes brightened. "A café! I can hardly wait. We need more restaurants in town."

She placed the water on the counter and pulled out her money. The seashells she'd collected clattered onto the counter with her change. "Sorry. I was out searching for shells."

"Oh, you won't find many around here," the woman told her. "We've got some, but the best and closest place to find them is about an hour away, on St. George Island."

She frowned. "I've never heard of it."

The clerk's eyes danced with delight. "That's because you're not from around here," she said in her elegant Southern drawl, "but you stick around a few months, and you'll learn all the tricks. I'm Shelby, by the way."

"Reece."

"We look about the same age."

"I'm twenty-five."

"Twenty-four. I'm helping my grandmother out with her gas station."

Reece peered around. "I haven't met her."

"You will. She's mostly here early mornings to get the breakfast going. But her health isn't that great."

Shelby's eyes darted to the counter, and Reece got the distinct feeling that she could use a friend same as her.

"How do you get to St. George Island?"

"It's just down the highway past Apalachicola."

"I don't know where any of that is," Reece said with a nervous laugh.

Shelby squinted at her. "Tell you what. My shift is almost over. If you can wait half an hour, I'll take you there myself."

Her heart ballooned at the thought of finding a friend. "I would like that."

* * *

The ride to St. George Island zoomed by faster than Reece had imagined. They drove past the sweet town of Port St. Joe and eventually past Apalachicola, taking a bridge over marshy water and then another bridge to St. George.

As soon as they were on the island proper, her eyes widened at the sight of a gleaming white tower. "They have their own lighthouse here, too?"

Shelby laughed. "Sure do. But this one's been rebuilt because the old one collapsed."

Reece found a certain poetic beauty in being rebuilt after falling apart. That was how she felt, like she needed to be rebuilt. But who would she be when the construction was complete?

Shelby chatted the whole drive down the main strip, which took them past houses atop lumber stilts and finally to an entrance for a state park. "This is the best shelling on the island. If you want better shells, you've got to take a boat to Little St. George," she said as they entered the gate and headed toward a parking lot. "And there's even better ones out the West Pass. But you gotta take a boat there, too."

White sands covered nearly every square inch of area. On the road opposite the beach stood tall pines and in front of them, large grassy sand dunes.

Reece followed Shelby to the beach, and her eyes nearly popped from her head at the many scattered shells on the sand. Some were nearly as large as her palm.

"Look at all those!"

"Sanibel is better," Shelby said. "But us locals are pretty proud of what we've got here. I could spend hours shell seeking, but I've got work." She sighed. "What about you? What work do you do?"

"Oh, I'm in medical school."

"Stop it," Shelby said, eyes wide.

"Yeah, at Tulane, but my dad died a few months ago, and so now I'm here helping my mom."

Her mouth dipped into a frown. "My parents both died when I was younger. My grandmother raised me."

"I'm sorry."

"Seems like we're sorry for each other." She grinned then. "Come on. Let's keep looking."

After an hour they stopped searching and headed back toward Apalachicola.

"If you're hungry, I know a great restaurant in town," Shelby said, pointing off the bridge toward the charming downtown.

Reece's stomach grumbled loudly and both women laughed. "I guess I am hungry."

They parked and headed inside the Seafood Grill, where Reece ordered the grouper and shrimp basket. While they waited for their food, the women chatted.

"You *look* smart," Shelby remarked. She spotted the confusion on Reece's face and added, "You just have a smart way about you."

"I look like a nerd, you mean," she corrected.

Her new friend's eyes narrowed. "No, not at all. You just look intelligent." She paused. "Do you not want to look smart?"

Reece considered that. She'd never really thought about it. But when faced with the question, she couldn't help but blurt out, "I want to look more like you, I guess. What I mean is, your hair and makeup are perfect. So are your clothes. You're like my sister. She makes leggings and oversize T-shirts look sexy. You do, too."

Shelby rested her chin on her knuckles. "You could, too. You're gorgeous. You just aren't using it. But trust me, even if you do use it, sometimes the man you're in love with doesn't notice."

She looked deflated and Reece tsked. "I very much doubt that you'd be interested in a man who wasn't crazy for you."

Shelby rolled her eyes. "You'd be surprised. But enough about me. Let's focus on you." Reece squirmed. *Did they have to?* "Let me guess— you've been so busy studying your whole life that you haven't had a chance to really explore fun stuff, girlie stuff."

Wow. She had hit the nail on the head. Reece's insides quivered at the realization. "That's it. I've always been so busy with school that I've never really taken the time to focus on me."

"And I'm not crazy about school at all, so I've had plenty of time to focus on myself," she said with a laugh. "Come on. When we finish lunch, we're going to have some fun."

And they did. Shelby dragged Reece into several local boutiques, one named Up the Street and the other was Apalach Outfitters. Apalach Outfitters was a mesh of outdoor branded T-shirts paired with boutique clothing for women. Reece immediately fell in love with the soft fabrics and muted, beachy colors.

"Oh my gosh, I love this," she said, holding up a soft white crop top and long linen pants.

"Get them," Shelby encouraged her. "They'll look great on you."

After shopping, Shelby instructed Reece to head to her house. She lived with her grandmother in a stilted cottage on the beach. It was only a short walk to the gas station. Her grandmother wasn't home, and Shelby dragged Reece into her bedroom, which was painted a light blue and had gauzy drapes over a sliding door that stepped out onto a deck with an amazing beach view.

"It's so beautiful here," Reece said. "Is that why you stayed?"

Shelby was pulling clothes from her closet. Her nose wrinkled. "A lot of my friends did move away. Some folks do, but most of them come back because there's something intoxicating about Sugar Cove. We love it here. It's just this little treasure that few tourists know about. But I stayed because my parents are gone, and Grandma needs the help."

Reece deflated from the sadness in Shelby's tone. "Is this what you want to do? The gas station?"

Her new friend shrugged. "I don't know. It's a good business, and I like the people. To be honest, I'm not sure what I want to do."

Join the club. She eyed the clothes that were piling high on the bed. "What are you doing?"

Shelby giggled. "I'm giving you a makeover."

"What?"

"Sit. The first thing we're doing is trimming your hair."

Reece possessively grabbed a hunk of her brown tendrils. "My hair?"

Shelby cocked her head. "I know what I'm doing. I cut my own hair. Grandma showed me. I can cut yours into long, beautiful layers that will frame your face."

She could? Reece glanced into a mirror and slowly pulled the ponytail holder from her hair. Long brown strands fell to her shoulders. Her hair had no body, no style. What was the worst thing that could happen? Shelby would butcher it?

But when she sneaked a peek at Shelby's strawberry tresses, she instantly knew that she was in good hands. She swallowed down the hard lump in her throat. "Okay. Let's do it."

Shelby squealed with glee and grabbed the scissors. "This is going to be fun."

* * *

An hour later Reece couldn't believe her eyes. Her normally straight tresses hung in soft waves to her shoulders. A delicate fringe of bangs framed her dark brows, and her eyes, accented in smoky gray and creamy taupe, had never looked better.

Shelby finished lining Reece's mouth and applying a coat of pale pink lipstick. "You have gorgeous lips—so full and pouty. Men love that kind of thing."

She rolled her eyes. Reece had never been good with guys. She got nervous around them and was so brainy she didn't know what to talk about other than medical stuff, which she didn't like anyway.

But when she took a second peek in the mirror, she barely recognized herself. Her lips *were* full and pouty. How had she never known that before?

"You need to come out with me some night," Shelby said. "Maybe I can even convince the guy I'm crazy about to come, too. Some folks from my high school get together every once in a while. It's fun. You might enjoy it."

Had Reece finally joined the cool kids' club without Chandler being the first invited? "Thanks. I'd like that."

Shelby rose and tossed some clothes at her. "See if these fit. They'd look great on you."

Reece ducked into the en suite bathroom and left the door cracked as she pulled off her T-shirt and shimmied into the silky blouse.

"How's living in the lighthouse?" Shelby asked.

"Cramped," she said with a laugh. "It's not very big."

"Oh, I thought you were talking about ghosts."

Reece opened the door and poked her head out. "Ghosts?"

Her friend laughed. "I'm only joking. There aren't any ghosts in the lighthouse. But there is a mystery."

She sucked air. "No."

"Mm hm. You done dressing?"

"Oh, no." Reece padded back into the belly of the bathroom, but she was not about to drop the conversation. "What's the mystery?"

"Well, it's said that a long time ago, maybe a hundred years ago or so, the lighthouse keeper was a widower with a daughter. Apparently the daughter loved a fisherman's son, but the fisherman and the lighthouse keeper hated one another."

Shelby paused and Reece couldn't stop herself from asking, "Why?"

"No clue. But they did. Well, one night there was a violent storm. It came up fast, and the fisherman was surprised by it. He got caught in the roaring waves. Well, every few hours the lighthouse lamp's wick had to be trimmed, which meant the light had to be put out. While the light was out, the fisherman shipwrecked along the rocks of the cape. When they got the light back on, the lighthouse keeper's daughter saw the mess and ran out to see if she could save the man she loved." Shelby paused dramatically before adding, "And she was never seen again. Neither of them was."

She sensed Shelby might have been pulling her leg. "Is that story true?"

"Hand to God, it is. Crazy, isn't it?"

"How'd you hear about it?"

"Oh, Aiden told me. He knows everything. His family's been settled here for generations."

"Aiden?"

"He's older. Not my want-to-be boyfriend." She laughed. "You done in there?"

Reece finished pulling on the buttery leggings that Shelby had given her. She took a long look in the mirror, nodded in appreciation, and then she stepped out into the bedroom.

Shelby released a low wolf whistle. "Reece Rigby, you are a knockout. You are most definitely going out with us next time."

Reece smiled widely. She felt beautiful. She didn't feel like a brainy medical school student who detested her course in life. She felt different, free.

"Thank you," she told her. "I mean it, really. Thank you for the hair and makeup. How can I repay you?"

Shelby wrinkled her nose. "You don't repay me. This is what friends do for one another." She rose from the bed. "Take the clothes. You're going to need them for your new life here."

Yes, Reece decided. She would need them. In the back of her mind the email that she'd received that morning from her professor became a distant memory even though she had to respond.

As she glanced at herself in the mirror once more, Reece knew this was the place she was supposed to be.

And then she remembered something. "Oh! I've got to go."

Shelby looked at her quizzically. "Why?"

Reece draped her purse over her shoulder and tucked her new clothes under one arm. "Because I made West Indies Salad and it's been marinating in the fridge for two days. I need to get home and see how it tastes."

CHAPTER 14
Chandler

"You going to try the salad?" her mother called from the kitchen.

Chandler had just finished laying out the last of the checkered cloths atop the tables. They were shiny and would wipe down easily, perfect for cleaning up spills.

She ran her hands over the cloth, smoothing out the last wrinkle. "Be right there."

After heading through the swinging doors, she found her sister and mother hunched over a glass bowl.

Reece looked like she was wearing new clothes and her hair was trimmed. "I like your hair."

A blush crept up her sister's cheeks. "Thank you. But let's get to business." She pulled off the plastic lid and smiled. "Here it is, West Indies Salad."

A symphony of cold crab meat and onions sat in the bowl. "How did you make it?"

"Well," Reece said proudly (was she wearing makeup?), "it's easy. Layers of lump crab and onions with oil, vinegar and ice water placed on top. The whole thing marinates for two days and then you eat it. Let me dish it out for you."

She drained the liquid in the sink and, using two forks, laid a small amount of the crab and onions on a plate for them to share.

Their mother handed Chandler a cracker. "Try it with this."

She forked a mound of crab onto the salty cracker and took a bite. She moaned in satisfaction. Light and delicately flavored crab was married with the thin layers of onion, adding to the sweet flavor and accentuating it.

"This is amazing."

"It's a well-known dish," her mother said. "I just didn't think to open with it. Reece did, though," she said, nodding to her daughter. "Honey, did you get a haircut?"

"I did. Shelby from the gas station gave it to me. And she told me about a mystery here in the lighthouse."

Chandler tilted her head. "What kind of mystery?"

And then Reece proceeded to tell them about a young woman and her forbidden love and a shipwreck.

When she finished, Chandler lifted her brows. "What a story. So romantic and tragic."

Her sister sighed. "I know. Apparently some guy named Aiden knows all about it."

Her mother stiffened and then quickly took another bite of the salad. "Honey, this is amazing. Our opening is going to rock."

The girls laughed at their mother's old-school slang. Chandler smiled. "It *is* going to rock, isn't it? Only a few more days now."

Her mother stabbed her fork into the salad. "Eat up. We've got a whole pound of this to get through so that Reece can prepare more for our grand day."

The three women laughed as they tucked into the delightful meal. Chandler sneaked a few glances at her sister and noticed that Reece was smiling wider than she'd seen her do in a long time.

Chandler only wished that she could feel that same joy.

* * *

It was two days until the opening of the Lighthouse Café and the past week had been a blur. There had been much more to do than Chandler had anticipated, what with getting a business license and having the city come out and inspect the kitchen to make sure everything was up to code.

It was all finished, and she had been so busy she'd barely had time to catch a breath.

She did, however, find a few moments to chat with Hudson, as she was doing now. "My mom says Sophie's show is in a week. Are you coming home to be a part of it?"

Chandler's insides shriveled. She still hadn't told him the truth. "There's a lot to do here."

He nodded at her, and she lovingly touched the screen where his jaw rested. "I understand. But from what you've said everything is pretty much running itself."

"If I leave now, she won't have anyone to help her. She hasn't hired staff."

"How about I come and bus tables?" he joked.

She shook her head. "Now I would love to see that—the brilliant and handsome Hudson Wheeler bussing tables like a broke college kid."

"I would be a broke college kid for you."

It felt like she'd been punched in the heart. Here he was being so honest, and she was keeping her secrets from him, hiding away her shame in the dark corners of her heart.

"I won't stay away too much longer," she promised even though she didn't know if it was the truth.

"You've never missed one of Sophie's jewelry shows."

"I don't think it'll break her heart if I'm absent from one."

"Even if you aren't there, I'll go to represent you. I haven't seen any of the pieces you gave her. You're so shy about your work, but it's always brilliant."

"No," she said quickly. "Don't go."

Hudson frowned. "Why not?"

Think, Chandler. "Because you don't have to do that. If I don't make it back in time, that is."

"I have the feeling you won't."

She tucked a strand of hair behind her ear nervously. She had to keep him away from that show. "You're busy. It's not a big deal. I can let you see the pieces later."

"After they're sold?" he reminded her flatly.

"I took pictures." She minimized the screen and scrambled to locate the pics of the jewelry that Sophie had denied. "I can show them to you."

"It's not the same. You know that. Under the gallery lights the jewels look better."

Oh no. Her insides were a twisted mess of angst. "I...I just prefer if we go together, and that you don't go alone. I know you're my biggest cheerleader, but this time it'll be okay."

His brown eyes searched her, and half a second later he said, "Okay. I won't go. If that's what you want."

The tightness in her chest loosened, and she could breathe again. "It's what I want."

"Then I'll give it to you."

Hudson would keep his promise. He always did. No longer worried about him discovering that Sophie hadn't accepted her into the show, Chandler nestled back against the covers on the small bed.

"Tell me about your day," she said.

He proceeded to tell her about a new client that he'd snagged for the law firm, but she was distracted, thinking of the show and how Sophie had denied her entry.

She wanted to lean on him and explain everything, and when he finished telling her about his day, he gave her an opening.

"You look like you've got something on your mind."

Here it was. Her chance to say that she was a failure.

But when Chandler opened her mouth, all that came out was, "I'm fine. There's just a lot to do."

She had to tell him the truth. But how? How could she tell the perfect man with the perfect life that he loved a woman who wasn't perfect at all?

CHAPTER 15

Ginny

T he next days moved briskly. She'd gotten her permits all in a row and ordered the food that was needed. The girls had been kept busy cleaning and prepping, and she had even managed to dodge every question about the house back in Buckhead, insisting that she'd simply sold the place under duress.

"Well, that's it," she declared, putting the last casserole in the fridge. "We're all set to open tomorrow. We only need to be up and baking the dishes first thing in the morning."

"And then I have to make the banana pudding," Reece said with a euphoric grin that made Ginny wonder if she missed Tulane at all.

Her daughter had slipped into the role of kitchen assistant with an ease that pleased yet worried her. Reece never discussed returning to school. But she was nothing if not responsible.

Her youngest slipped an oven glove over one hand. "The West Indies salad is also ready. But I'll confess that I built one small casserole last night, just for us to taste test." She opened the oven door and settled the small steel pan on the counter. A creamy white casserole sprinkled with browned breadcrumbs bubbled cheerfully before them. She produced a fork from the drawer. "Want a bite?"

"Yes, please." Ginny took the fork her daughter offered and slid it into the Tasty Chicken Casserole.

It was the perfect name for the dish, because it outshone every other chicken casserole that she had ever consumed. Filled with chicken that had been oven-baked until the skin was a crisp golden brown and the meat pulled away from the bone, they had chopped it and tossed it with a mixture of boiled eggs, creamy soup, and rice. The result, once it sat overnight to allow the flavors to mingle, was a symphony of delight.

She blew on her fork to cool the serving before biting into the casserole. She wiggled her body in cheer. The celery added crunch, while the soup created a creamy overall texture that filled her with *all the feels*. This was comfort food at its cozy and warmest.

Surely beach-living folks could appreciate that. But even so, Ginny worried about her choice of dish for opening day.

Before she could convey her doubts, Reece took a bite and moaned. "This is delicious."

She brightened. "Do you think so?"

"Yes. Perfect for tomorrow. You've got the light West Indies Salad and then this for anyone who wants something heartier. You know how men like big food."

Ginny laughed. "Yes, I suppose so."

Chandler walked in then, her purse slung over one shoulder. She'd been amazing these past weeks, helping with the marketing to get the word out about the restaurant.

But still, she noticed that every time her oldest didn't think she was being watched, her mouth dipped into a frown. She wasn't like Reece, who was bold and emotional. Chandler buried her feelings, and she had been close to Jack. Ginny suspected his death was affecting her eldest more than she wanted to admit.

Her daughter smiled, but sadness lingered in her eyes. "Y'all ready?"

"Would you like a taste first?"

"Yes." Ginny handed her a fork and Chandler blew on the hot casserole before delicately placing it on her tongue. "Amazing. You're opening is going to be so great, Mama." They munched for a few minutes. "Are y'all ready?"

"I'm ready for a girl's afternoon out," she exclaimed.

"You deserve it for how hard you've worked," her oldest told her. "I'm proud of you. Everything looks beautiful."

She took a moment to appreciate the dining room. They'd painted it a soft lemon with a ring of robin's egg blue at the top and another strip halfway up the wall. The cane-backed chairs had been polished until light refracted from their surfaces, and atop the tables lay red-and-white-checkered cloths, a perfect final touch that added a bit of familiarity and warmth to the room.

The café smelled of lemon and a grandmother's kitchen—sugar and yeast, which was the way Ginny hoped to keep it.

"Let's get our things," she said. "Reece, did you turn off the oven?"

Reece snapped her fingers and whirled around. "Almost forgot." She flipped the knob and frowned. "It's sticking at the top and not wanting to dial down. Oh, there, I got it." She looked up and grinned. Let's go shopping."

Outside, the sun was bright and hot, as it should have been at the beach. The air smelled of brine, and the humidity made Ginny feel like she was being wrapped in a blanket. Most people hated it, especially in the summer, but as the season was quickly turning into fall, she found the humidity reminded her of the new life she was quickly learning to embrace.

They drove into Port St. Joe and stopped to eat lunch at Uptown Bar and Grill, where they split smoked tuna dip and a low country boil. The smoky flavor from the tuna dip ignited Ginny's senses, and she immediately fell in love with it.

When they'd eaten all they could, they walked around downtown.

Reece boldly strode in front of them, exploring the town like a three-year-old on steroids. That was her, always leading the way with punch.

With her so far ahead, Ginny decided it was a good time to pick Chandler's brain. "Everything okay?"

She nodded absently. "Sure."

"Do you think I'm moving too quickly with the restaurant?"

Her eyes flared with surprise. "No, I don't think so. I mean, at first I was worried since you never told us you were going to sell the house. But I see you here, at the lighthouse, and I know this is your place, Mama. This was what you were meant to do. I only wish Dad was here to see it."

Her jaw tightened. "Well, I'm sure he's watching us from wherever he is." Which was more than likely South of the Border. She squeezed her daughter's hand tightly. "If you ever want to talk about anything, please come to me. You and your father were close. I don't want you to feel as if you can't talk to me about him."

Her gaze slid to the corner of her eye. "I know, Mama. I'm okay."

But she wasn't. Anyone could see that. "How's Hudson?"

"Dying for me to come home," she gushed.

"You can return whenever you like. Day after tomorrow if you want. Oh, that reminds me. A package came for you."

Chandler's face snapped toward her mother. "A package?"

"Yes, I left it in the dining room. Forgot to tell you," she said by way of apology.

"That's okay."

"Is it something from Hudson?"

Her face crumpled. "No, I don't think so."

"Well, I had to sign for it, so it must be important."

Reece gave a passing glance over her shoulder to them. "Let's go into that secondhand store—Sisters Consignment." She pointed across the street. "It looks cute."

They strolled over. After all, there was no rush. They didn't have deadlines or a country club dinner to rush off to. Ginny loved the laid-back quality of her new life, even if she burned with anger whenever her thoughts drifted to Jack and That Woman, which was nearly every hour.

When they entered the shop, she was surprised to find it was very much more than an upscale thrift store. Sunlight poured through the windows, splashing onto cerulean blue pottery and glinting off antique porcelain dishes. Leather wingback chairs, lamps and bric-a-brac were sprinkled throughout the racks of upscale designer clothing.

"Welcome! How can I hel— Ginny Crawford, is that you?"

She had been running her fingers down a lovely sea-blue cashmere sweater when the sound of her maiden name made her heart jump. She peered into the face of the woman who'd clearly recognized her and replied, "Molly Lindsey?"

"Oh, my goodness, it is you! Yes, it's me, Molly. Come here and give me a hug."

Molly—whom she had not seen in over twenty years—wore a bright blue linen shirtdress accessorized with glittery gold and silver chains. Her jewelry clinked as she pulled Ginny into a bear hug that she couldn't help but melt into. Relief at seeing a familiar—if distant—face warmed her heart. There was comfort in seeing Molly, even though it had been years since they'd been in the same room.

Adding to it was the fact that her old friend smelled of gardenias and vanilla. Ginny figured she smelled of low country boil.

When Molly pulled away, she said, "Ginny, you look absolutely beautiful, exactly as you did when we were in college."

"So do you," she told her and meant it.

Molly's blonde hair was painted with white highlights. She looked as if she spent every free day lazing on the beach.

"Are you visiting the Port?" she asked.

"No, I've moved. I bought the lighthouse."

"No!" She clapped her hands with surprise. "You're the one opening the restaurant? The Lighthouse Café?"

A bashful grin crept over Ginny's face. "That's me."

"How wonderful."

She turned to her girls. "Come and meet Molly Lindsey. Oh, you're not Lindsey anymore, though."

"Oh, I'm back to being a Lindsey. But that's a story for another time. Let me meet your beautiful daughters."

"Girls, Molly and I were sorority sisters in college. We were Kappas together. This is Chandler and Reece."

"Well, you two are just gorgeous." Molly patted both girls on the arms. "Just as beautiful as your mother."

Her gaze roamed over the store. "Is this your shop?"

"Yes, you remember I'm from the area?"

"Right. It's been so long."

Molly waved her hands, motioning to the entire store. "My mama started it, and I came to help. Her health's not that great."

"You've got a sister, right?" she asked.

She rolled her eyes. "Yes, but that's another one of those conversation for a different time." She paused to take in Ginny and grinned wide. "I'm just so tickled you're here. When's your opening day? I'm gonna be first in line for a meal."

The two women spoke for a few minutes as she filled Molly in on details about the store. They exchanged numbers and promised to get together.

Ginny walked out of Sisters Consignment with a lopsided grin invading her mouth. She was elated to reconnect with Molly. If her opening day went as well as today, she would be overflowing with happiness.

The only question was—would it?

CHAPTER 16

Chandler

T he box sat in her lap. Its very presence seemed accusatory, as if Chandler had involuntarily committed a crime.

After getting home from the outing with her mom and sister, she had spied the box atop a checker-clothed table. She knew immediately what it was, and her stomach clenched in worry.

She'd never given Sophie her address at the beach, but the gallery owner was wily and probably got it from Hudson's mom, who got it from him.

Sweat sprouted on her brow. Sophie wouldn't tell Hudson's mom about Chandler's absence in the show. The gallery owner was much too discreet for that. Besides, Hudson needed to hear from Chandler that she wouldn't be in it—and she needed to tell him soon.

She would. Just not today. If she remembered correctly, the show was next Thursday. There was time to tell him still.

She took the box off the table.

"I'm going to warm up some casserole for dinner," Reece announced.

"Thanks."

Perfect. That meant she would have the bedroom all to herself.

She entered the room and locked the door to the small room that the three women had thrown together for her and Reece. They'd found not-too-battered mattresses and, and after a good wash in scalding water, the sheets released the musty smell that had seemed to clutch to them with desperation.

She slid a kitchen knife under the packing tape and held her breath. Chandler peeled back the cardboard to find the box filled with balls of tissue paper enclosed in bubble wrap.

Sophie had packaged each piece individually, and for that, she was grateful, because none of the stones would be damaged during shipping.

She sifted through the loose paper until her hands circled around the largest piece. She dug her finger into the bubble wrap and tugged it away until the velvet bag lay exposed. She slid the necklace from the bag and pushed the box away. Chandler carefully straightened the delicate gold chain that she had built link by link. Both ends of the chain met a stone —on the left a squarely cut watermelon tourmaline and on the right, a sapphire in a matching shape. Between those stones and attached with gold wire, lay other flat and square jewels. The entire piece was a mosaic, reminiscent of an abstractly designed stained glass window. She held it up, and light pierced the stones, bringing the entire piece to life.

There was no doubt about it—the piece was gorgeous. Color danced atop the surface. It was a piece a woman would love to add to her spring collection. Yes, certain pieces of jewelry were to be worn in certain seasons.

But as much as Chandler acknowledged all of that, her heart still sank because she knew that Sophie had been right.

Though it was beautiful, the jewelry lacked originality, personality, the touch that Chandler had imbued in her earlier pieces. It was cold, lifeless, and it was with heavy sadness that she realized Sophie had made the correct decision in omitting her work from the show.

Having such lifeless pieces on display wouldn't have helped her reputation as a goldsmith.

As hard as it was to admit, she had to accept that even *if* she wanted to keep creating, she didn't have anything new to say or add to her work. She was finished as a designer before the age of thirty.

She fell back onto the bed with a hard plop.

The doorknob jiggled and Chandler sat up. She gently wrapped the necklace back up and placed it inside the box before crossing to the door and opening it.

"Sorry about that," she said to Reece.

Her sister's gaze scoured over the room, landing on the box. "Do you need some alone time?"

"No. I'm fine."

Frown lines wrinkled Reece's forehead, but she said nothing.

Chandler sank back onto the bed and closed her eyes. Her light was gone. The light of inspiration that had guided her these past few years.

It had vanished. What would she do with her life now?

CHAPTER 17

Ginny

O n opening day, the bedside alarm chirped her awake at five thirty in the morning. She lay in bed a moment, trying to register the intense sensation coming from her stomach.

It felt like a thousand butterflies were skimming the walls of her belly, while pinpricks of excitement sparked from her fingertips. In the darkness she grinned.

She couldn't wait to get into her kitchen.

She tiptoed from her bed and showered as quietly as possible, doing her best not to wake the girls. Reece had said she would be in the kitchen at six thirty to prep the dessert, and Chandler would help around that time as well, doing any last-minute tasks before they opened the doors at eleven.

After showering, she pulled her hair into a ponytail and headed into the kitchen. The steel-paneled refrigerators gleamed and hummed, seeming to whisper that they were as ready as she was to bring new life back into the lighthouse.

She pulled the casseroles from the fridge and turned on the oven. The gas cavern usually warmed quickly, which had been a pleasant surprise the first time she used it.

While waiting for the oven to get to temp, she retrieved the ingredients Reece would need for the banana pudding. After that, she scooped dollops of West Indies Salad into cups of Bibb lettuce and arranged them on individual porcelain plates before encasing them in plastic wrap. Ginny had no idea how many people to expect. She didn't want to delude herself and fix one hundred plates of salad, so she settled on twenty. If there was salad left over, that would be fine. She and the girls would enjoy it for supper.

Ten minutes passed, which meant the oven would be ready for the chicken casseroles. She opened the door and froze as fright pooled in her chest.

The oven was cold. Not warm. There wasn't even a hint of a temperature change.

She checked the knobs. Maybe she'd turned on a burner instead of the oven. No. The burner knobs hadn't been touched. The only knob to be twisted out of place was the single shiny black circle that controlled the oven.

Oh God. What would she do?

Fear crawled inside her bones and threatened to declare squatter's rights. Her chest tightened and her breathing came in small, quick inhalations.

She was panicking. A thousand thoughts fired inside her head. *It is opening day. How could this happen to me? Why did I ever think I could make it on my own? Where is Jack? He always solved our problems.*

The last thought sent a thunderbolt to her heart. It jolted her from falling into the mire of her predicament.

Jack wasn't here. It was because of his selfishness that Ginny *was* here. She had faced worse crises in her life than a broken oven.

There were options. She only had to think.

It took a moment longer than she would've liked, but a solution flared in her mind.

She flipped off the oven knob, picked up a casserole and headed to the front door. Ginny unlocked it and stepped outside.

One of the beauties about the beach, and something she couldn't get over, was how much *sky* her eyes took in at night. There weren't trees to cloud her view of the heavens.

She got to enjoy the constellated darkness and would have in that moment if she hadn't been charging toward the gas station.

The sun was beginning to break on the horizon. A thin band of gold rimmed the sky as far as her eyes could see.

To her left was a slope of patchy grass and sugary sand that trailed down to the beach.

It was from that direction that a very masculine yet velvety voice said, "Now why are you running around at daybreak delivering casseroles that look much too heavy to carry?"

Her heart jumped and she whipped left. Standing in a halo of sunrise like an angel (or a devil, because she was still unsure how she felt about him), was Aiden.

He slumped onto one hip from walking up the slope, and he looked completely at ease and relaxed, while she felt frazzled from head to foot.

He pointed to the pan. "Can I help you carry it?"

"No," she snapped and watched as he rocked back. Quickly realizing how defensive she sounded, Ginny exhaled, and her shoulders sagged in defeat. "I'm sorry. My oven's broken. On the opening day of my restaurant."

"Broken? Now how am I supposed to enjoy that delicious casserole?"

She smiled tightly. "I was hoping the ladies at the gas station might help me out and cook it."

"They might." Light bled over the horizon quickly, and a golden glow splashed across Aiden's face. His warm eyes took her in, and a faint smile traced his lips. "But I could do you one better."

His tone sent a flame dancing down Ginny's spine. What was wrong with her? The oven was broken, her opening day ruined and she was being charmed by his eyes?

He extended both hands. "Here. Let me take it."

She swiveled toward the gas station. "But..."

"I've been around an oven or two. Maybe it's an easy fix."

Was he really offering to help? At daybreak? When all she'd ever done was sling acidic words at him? Well, that wasn't *all*. She had been nice when they first met, before the auction began and he bid against her.

"While you're standing here, that casserole's aging," he reminded her.

She handed him the dish and led him into the lighthouse. Soon as he stepped inside, he stopped and sniffed. "How long did you leave the oven on?"

"Maybe five, ten minutes."

He rested the pan on a table. "Let's open some windows."

Ginny sniffed and could've pinched herself for not detecting the scent of gas earlier. "I was so busy prepping, I didn't smell it," she said by way of apology.

"Good thing you ran into me, then." He gave her a warm smile and pushed open a window. "Let's open the door, too." When all the windows were open and the overhead fan was whirling, pushing the gas-laced air out of the building, he turned to her with a lopsided smile. "Now. Where's the oven?"

He followed her into the kitchen. "That's it."

He opened the door and peeked inside so far that his head disappeared. His left hand rested on the outside edge of the oven, and she noticed, to her own annoyance, that Aiden's ring finger lay bare.

She glanced down at hers. Bare, also. She'd tossed both rings into her purse while driving down I-65. The temptation to hurl them out the open window had gnawed at her. But the set was much too valuable to simply trash.

Aiden's voice tugged her from the memory. "Do you have a lighter?"

"Yes, there's one here somewhere." She dug in a drawer and located the long, slender tool. "Found it."

She placed it in his open hand. The lighter disappeared into the oven. It clicked on and then Aiden rose and shut the door. "What temperature would you like it on?"

"Um, three-fifty."

He turned the dial and opened the door. A smile broke out on his face, and Aiden tipped his head to Ginny. "Voila! Oven fixed."

Her heart leaped. "Really?"

"Really."

She peeked inside to see a flame spread out across the back. "How did you...?"

"The pilot light went out. That was all." He handed her the lighter, and their fingers brushed as she took it. Aiden stood only a foot from her, and for the first time Ginny's eyes drank him in.

He was nearly a foot taller than her, with warm brown eyes and golden skin. When Aiden smiled (like he was doing now), the corners of his eyes fanned. His salt-and-pepper hair was cut just long enough for it to curl at his neck, though Ginny had the feeling it didn't take a lot for it to be windswept, and she suspected that it lived mostly in such a wonderfully lazy state.

He smelled of soap and salt, the scents as familiar to her as a cozy blanket. Little pricks danced on her fingers, and it was only then that Ginny realized they were still touching. Both of their hands were still wrapped around the lighter.

She felt a rush of heat flame her cheeks, and she took the lighter as he released it. "Thank you." The words slipped from her lips in a whisper, and she cleared a frog from her throat, hoping the sound would also rip away the cobwebs that had clearly clouded her brain.

All it took was the simple touch of a man and she couldn't think. What was wrong with her? But the truth was, Jack had displayed very little affection for her their last few years together. His fingers coldly touching her shoulder was as intimate as they'd been for months. Her relationship with Jack had evaporated well before his death.

"Thank you," she repeated, this time finding her voice. "You saved my opening day. Come back and your lunch is on the house as a thank-you for your help."

His lips parted into a warm smile. "I appreciate it, but I'm going to pay. It's the least I can do for ruining your life."

Ginny bristled, but she quickly spotted the glint of amusement in his eyes. "You didn't ruin my life."

"Hope not. But that's the impression I got last time we met on the beach." He grazed past her, leaving behind his scent—the ocean and soap. "I'd hate to be on the hook for ruining a life, especially when the woman inhabiting it is so lovely."

Her cheeks burned like red-hot pokers straight from a fire. All she could do was stare as Aiden strode from her kitchen and out the door.

CHAPTER 18

Ginny

A fter Aiden left, her head swam in confusion. She found herself shamefully attracted to him. She didn't want to be drawn to such an obviously arrogant man. Because he was arrogant, wasn't he?

There was little time to ponder such things because Reece bounded into the kitchen, smiling brightly. She'd scrubbed her face, leaving her cheeks rosy, and her wet hair was tied back into a tight bun.

"Ready for opening day?" she asked with an exuberance that made her smile.

Ginny placed the chicken casserole in the now warm oven. "I sure am."

"Let me just make sure the tables don't need another wipe down." Her daughter disappeared into the dining room, and when she returned, she said, "Why're the windows open?"

Ginny, embarrassed by her mistake and not feeling comfortable sharing any details about Aiden, headed toward the door. "I just wanted some sea air in here for a minute. I'll close them."

She yanked open the fridge and piled milk and eggs into her arms. "Okay. Who's ready for some banana pudding?"

* * *

By the time the Lighthouse Café opened its doors officially at eleven a.m. on the dot, a line of customers wound down the sidewalk and out into the parking lot.

Chandler scurried to the door and beamed. "Y'all ready?"

Reece grasped Ginny's hand. "Are you, Mama?"

Her heart ping-ponged in her chest. It was now or never. She gave a hard nod. "I'm ready. Let them in."

Chandler flipped the lock. "Okay, here we go."

She opened the door, and they helped seat the guests. The menu had been marker-drawn in Chandler's beautiful looping handwriting on a whiteboard.

Ginny grabbed the third party in line, and to her surprise, she saw it was her old friend Molly Lindsey and her mother.

"Told you I'd be here," Molly said, giving her a hug. "This is Cora, my mother."

Cora's lined face puckered sourly. "Pleased to meet you," she growled in a voice that suggested she was anything but.

Ginny spotted the cane that Cora gripped, and she instantly realized the elderly woman was probably in ill health.

"It's wonderful to meet you," she gushed. "Let's find you a table."

She quickly explained the way the menu worked—there were three courses and that's what you got, all three.

Her old sorority sister clapped excitedly. "I'm just so happy to see you and try these dishes."

The tables filled quickly, leaving the three women to their tasks of serving the guests. As Ginny glanced around the dining room, her heart inflated with cheer. Every single seat sat occupied. She hoped her twelve thirty lunch service elicited the same support from the locals.

She was just about to hang the placard that informed patrons the current lunch service was full and to try the next one, when a shadow stretched across the door.

Her eyes darted up and latched onto Aiden's. In the sunlight his bright blue eyes reminded her of chipped sapphires. Her throat tightened and she swallowed down the knot that had formed in it.

He smiled and the corners of his eyes fanned. Ginny's gaze cut away from him as she felt a flush creep up her neck.

"Sorry, I'm late," he explained. "Work kept me longer than I planned. Is there room for one more?"

She glanced over her shoulder. "The dining room's full."

His hopeful expression fell, and she cringed. She refused to turn him away after he saved her opening day.

Ginny cocked her head. "Come on. I have an idea."

He followed her to the kitchen. One counter was clear of food, and she pulled a free chair to it. "Will this work?"

Aiden smiled again. "This'll be just fine."

He ordered an iced tea, and Ginny brought him the West Indies Salad. While he ate, she wiped down another counter.

"West Indies salad," he said, delight in his voice. "Been a long time since I've had this."

She brightened. "You know it?"

"Mm hm. My mom used to make it on special occasions." He took a bite and slowly turned to her, his blue eyes shining. "Don't tell my mama, but this is better than hers."

She pressed a hand to her neck. "You flatter me."

"Not at all." He paused, considering the food. "I forgot to tell you earlier, but the place turned out nice. I'd ask what brought you here, but I got a feeling the day of the auction that it was nothing good."

"I was...out of sorts. My husband died recently."

"I'm sorry."

She shook her head. "It's a complicated tale."

Her daughters entered the kitchen. They stopped, Reece digging her heels into the floor, and both girls stared openly at their mother. They must've been wondering why Ginny was talking to a man.

She introduced them and Reece exclaimed. "Are you the *Aiden* who knows about the lighthouse love story?"

He chuckled. "I do. I know it. My family's been in Sugar Cove a long time."

"I've got to hear it," she said. "Is there really a ghost?"

He smiled. "I don't know about that."

She exhaled. "Good. I don't want a ghost. So...what do you do?"

Ginny flicked her away. "Later, Reece. Let the man eat his lunch. Plus, we've got tables to serve."

"Yeah, Reece," Chandler said, sauntering out the swinging doors.

Her daughter deflated, but she shot Aiden a look as she picked up a pitcher of tea. "I've got to hear what you know."

"Reece, let the man eat," she scolded again. Then her gaze dropped to his plate of chicken casserole. "Do you like it?"

He took a bite and moaned in a way that sent tingles down her spine. "Delicious. I love comfort food."

"Let's hope other people do, too." She peeked out of the porthole in the swinging door. Nearly every table she glanced at, there sat an empty plate, one scraped clean. It made her stomach tighten with hope. "I just hope folks don't mind eating things other than seafood."

"Looks like you've got a healthy crowd. But as for the menu, you should trust your gut." His gaze cut to Reece. "But as for what I do, I'm semi-retired."

"From what?" she inquired, leaning in.

Ginny wanted to bury her head in the sand. "Let's not disturb our guest."

"No one's disturbing me," he told her. "I'm retired from deep-sea treasure hunting."

Both their jaws dropped.

Her daughter pulled over a chair and sat beside Aiden. "Tell me everything."

He chuckled. "It's a lot of story. How about I save it for another day when I take the three of y'all out on my boat?"

"That sounds amazing," she told him, beaming.

Ginny was relieved that Reece was no longer being rude to him. "Oh, looks like we've got folks wanting to pay."

Her daughter took the hint, scurrying to clean tables and ring up the guests.

She served Aiden his dessert and then took a few minutes to make the rounds at the tables, talking to patrons and asking about their experience. Overwhelmingly people gushed that they loved the entire meal and couldn't wait to return tomorrow to see what she offered next.

Her body hummed with happiness as she cleaned plates and wiped down tables. It was only when Aiden came up to the register to pay that Ginny remembered he was even there.

"What did you think?" she asked, feeling her insides squirm. Why did his opinion matter so much?

He patted his flat stomach. "I thought it was fantastic. You're my new favorite restaurant."

"Thank you," she replied, grinning so widely that her cheeks ached.

"And I meant what I said," he told her.

"About what?"

"About having the three of y'all on my boat. It would be my pleasure."

In that moment Aiden's gaze latched onto hers, and she felt a stirring in her stomach, a tiny prickle of energy that she hadn't felt in years.

"I would...I would like that."

He took her number, and the whole while Ginny's gaze washed over Aiden, really studying him. There was a familiarness about his very presence, like a warm blanket, one she wanted to wrap around her body and press her nose into.

Right before he walked out the door, he said, "It's a date, then."

Ginny's stomach dropped. Was it a date? Then she laughed to herself. Of course, it wasn't. Her daughters would be there.

But what if it was? Was she ready for that?

* * *

"Here's to a successful opening day." Reece lifted her glass filled with a pale golden wine. "Congrats, Mama."

Ginny felt a band of love wind around her heart. "It was a success, wasn't it?"

Reece kicked her feet up on the table draped in a checkered cloth. "You filled up both lunch services, and people licked their plates clean."

She scoffed. "Oh, I don't know about that."

"No, she's right, Mama. I watched a man lift his plate and wipe his tongue over it," Chandler joked.

She playfully swatted her daughter. "Very funny. But are we ready for tomorrow?"

"We sure are." Reece lifted her glass in triumph. "The crab and artichoke casseroles are fixed, along with the corn pudding."

She smiled warmly. "And I've put together all the broccoli salads."

"And I watched while you also made the Coca-Cola cake," Chandler teased. The women laughed and she lifted her glass. "What? I'm not a cook."

"Hudson'll be surprised when he finally proposes," she joked. Worry flashed in her daughter's eyes. "Honey, is something wrong?"

"No. Yes." She exhaled a gusty sigh. "Yes, actually a lot is wrong."

A timer from the kitchen dinged, and Reece popped up from her seat. "Hold that thought. Let me grab the appetizer."

She had made hot crab dip for them to snack on. When she brought back the dip, it was bubbling hot, the top of it a lovely golden brown. It made her dizzy to think of all the recipes she had yet to explore from the cookbook. If this dip tasted as good as it looked, she would be elated.

While they waited for it to cool, she turned to Chandler. "Is this about the package you received the other day?"

She deflated onto the table, head and hands down. "It is. I'm ruined."

"What?" Alarm built inside of Ginny. "What do you mean?"

And then Chandler sat up with a loud intake of breath and revealed exactly what had been in the box and how she was finished as a jewelry designer. She had no spark, felt no joy for it.

She retrieved the box from her room and delicately unwrapped the fragile pieces of stone and gold. Ginny marveled at her daughter's gift. How could Chandler think that she was talentless when clearly she was anything but?

She lifted a necklace and stared at the delicate gold wire wrapping around the stones. Only a gifted goldsmith could have painstakingly created the golden chain and soldered the jewels to the gold bezels. The gems glinted under the light and the gold brightened.

Chandler stared into the box with eyes glassy from tears that had yet to spill. "And the worst part is that Hudson doesn't know. I haven't told him. He still thinks I'm in Sophie's show."

Ginny frowned. "You're not?"

She exhaled. "That's the reason I have all these. Sophie sent them back. She wouldn't take them."

"Aw, honey, I'm so sorry. But don't you think you should tell Hudson? He would want to support you."

Chandler squeezed her mother's hand before pulling away. "He's the biggest part of my New York artist existence. Seeing him, *telling* him means admitting my failure. How can I return to New York when no one will buy my art?"

Her heart broke. Here she was rejoicing in the start of a new life, and all the while Chandler felt as if hers was crumbling at her feet.

Well, if there was a feeling that she knew, it was having her life destroyed in a matter of seconds.

She dipped the serving spoon into the dip and dished it out onto plates as she carefully constructed an answer to her daughter. Ginny didn't think it right to dismiss her insecurities, but guiding her would be the best thing.

She handed a plate to Chandler, who took it with a muffled, "Thank you."

"Darling girl, you are so very gifted. If your art has left you, and you feel that you don't have it right now, stay here. Remain in Sugar Cove with me for as long as you like. Let Hudson come visit. See him. But I know he loves you and he doesn't think you're a failure."

"Maybe not," she muttered.

"I know he doesn't," she said softly. "Your father always believed in you girls. Both of y'all. You with your art and Reece, he trusted in your undeveloped talents as a doctor. He knew that both of you were capable of so much. But sometimes," here she took a moment to bite into a cracker topped with dip, "we all need to take a step back and survey our lives from a different perspective."

Ginny didn't know if she'd made any sense. All she knew was that this place, Sugar Cove, and this lighthouse were healing her. Months ago she never would have thought she'd have the talent or ability to open a restaurant and have a successful opening day, yet here she was.

Chandler's eyes were fixed on her plate of food and Ginny felt the need to give her a break from all the focus, so she turned to Reece. "And what about school? Any word on when you'll be starting in the summer? Or is it too early to ask?"

Her gaze, too, was pinned on the dish as she replied, "Nope. No word yet." Her gaze snapped up suddenly. "But I have a question for you."

"Yes?"

"How do you know Aiden?"

Her own gaze darted to the plate of food in front of her. "If you must know—"

"We must," Reece chirped.

Ginny ran her fingers through her hair. She always fiddled with it when words escaped her tongue. But it wasn't a lack of words that caused her to fidget. It was remembering the way he had looked at her.

It was too soon to date anyone, she reminded herself. Jack was barely cold in his grave.

"He saved the restaurant this morning."

Reece raked her fork through the dip. "He what?"

She felt a buoy of confidence now. "The pilot light was off, and I didn't catch it. I grabbed the casserole and was going to head across the street to see if they'd bake it at the gas station. But he was on the beach. He said he'd look at the oven and voila! He fixed it. End of story."

"He's a treasure hunter," Reece told Chandler as if it was a big secret.

"Used to be," she corrected. "At least that's what he said."

Chandler scraped a cracker across her plate, sweeping dip onto it. "Seems you know an awful lot about this man for someone you don't know."

She swatted her away. "I met him the day I bought the lighthouse. He's very arrogant, I can tell you that much. And he seems cocky, as well as dismissive. He's walked away from me a couple of times. Who does that? Walks away without properly ending a conversation?"

The girls exchanged a look. Chandler lifted her brows while Reece shook her head.

"Only handsome treasure hunters do such things," Reece told her. "And pirates."

Her other daughter frowned. "It's too early to talk about handsome men."

And there Ginny had the answer she already knew. Both girls knew the best of their father, and they expected her to mourn him like a devastated widow. Which she could.

"He did invite us onto his boat," Ginny said.

"Treasure hunting? I'm going," Reece announced. "Don't worry, Mama. I'll tell him we accept his date."

She laughed. "I appreciate that."

"No problem." Reece jumped up when another timer chimed from the kitchen. She clapped her hands. "Now. Who wants some cake?"

* * *

After the women cleaned up, Ginny was dog-tired. Her legs hurt; her neck hurt. But the ache felt good, like it was deserved after a long day's work.

As she kneaded her shoulder muscles, she swept past the entrance to the lighthouse tower. She paused and flipped on a light, instantly illuminating the stairwell.

Today had been a success. Could she add one more to it? Could she creep up and glance out at the shoreline? She placed her foot on the bottom step and stopped as worry and fear swallowed her.

No, not today. She couldn't make the trip. She snapped off the light and sighed.

But when would she be able to do it?

CHAPTER 19

Reece

The emails pinged on her phone at least once every few days. There had been so many at first that Reece had disabled notifications. She didn't want her mother to sneak a look at the contents.

But as Reece lay on the lumpy mattress after dinner, she opened her email and felt her body immediately stiffen. Her advisor had sent two emails already that week, asking for updates on her and honestly saying that if Reece didn't reply, the school would look upon that as her unenrolling from the program.

She wanted to go to summer school. Well, honestly, she didn't, but she wanted to *want* to go. She felt overly childish running from her problems. All Reece had to do was open one single email and reply, say she needed to begin the paperwork to take a break from Tulane, plead that she didn't want to be removed from the student roster, just be rolled over to restart in two semesters.

But every time she started to reply, every time her finger tapped the blue arrow to send, her stomach clenched up. Her entire body screamed that was not her path, but even her mother's words about her dad made guilt wash over her—that he knew Reece would become a brilliant doctor. It was what he had hoped for her future.

She glanced over at her purse, the purse that held *the pen*. The banana-shaped bag seemed to breathe, to expand and deflate from the overbearing presence of the pen.

She dropped her phone onto the mattress and pushed herself up. She grabbed the purse and riffled through it until her fingers brushed the cold metal. The pen had weight. It was a heavy instrument and not one that she would ever use in class to take notes with, but for day-to-day tasks it was perfect.

A perfect reminder of her failure.

"You will go to medical school and be a doctor," her father had said.

He'd pushed the idea on her from an early age. Reece sometimes wondered if her father had been so insistent on her path because she hadn't been born a boy and he'd always wanted a son who would become a doctor.

It worsened her guilt, the fact that he was gone now. Reece knew she should reply to her advisor's emails, say that she intended to return during the summer and make up what she'd missed. Or simply ask for the year off—see if she could return next fall.

Yet she lacked the motivation to do it.

She had too much energy to lie around, so she rose and headed into the kitchen, slipping past her mother's room. She spotted her sister outside watching the waves, and Reece considered going out to talk to her, but she knew Chandler well enough to realize that she wanted to be alone.

Ever since their father had died, it seemed as if they'd fallen apart. Reece was failing; Chandler's muse had up and vanished. The only person who was doing well was their mother, and she hadn't even admitted to having the house for sale.

Her life had taken so many new turns that Reece wanted comfort. She longed for stability.

She spotted the cookbook sitting on the table. She peeled back the delicate cover and flipped through the chapter headings until she reached the section she was looking for.

She quicky gathered flour, yeast, sugar and spread them out before her on the counter. Cooking, creating, was the one thing that filled her heart right now. She didn't want to languish in misery.

She wanted to bake.

She flipped to a cinnamon roll recipe and began by dissolving the yeast in warm water. She scanned the recipe while the yeast activated, creating bubbles on the water's surface.

She melted shortening in a pan with milk and sugar. She scanned more recipes while it cooled. Then she beat eggs and added it to the mixture. Finally she was ready to make dough. She scooped cups of flour into a bowl and stirred in the softened yeast. She added flour until the mixture was stiff and poured it out onto the counter, where she punched and kneaded, working it into gluten, or so she'd seen on several cooking shows.

She worked her frustration into the dough until it was pounded enough. Then she rounded it into a ball, dropped it into a bowl and covered it to let it rise.

She brushed flour from her hands and paused. What to do now? Without hesitating, Reece poured over the cookbook again, flipping to the cake section. She quickly found a simple pound cake and started once more. She whipped butter and sugar together, beat in eggs and added sifted flour. She added vanilla and almond extract to the mixture and inhaled deeply. The comforting scents reminded her of why she was doing this. They helped to shove away the knots of worry and guilt that had hardened in her shoulders. Knots created because she would be letting her dead father down by not pursuing the path that he had wanted for her.

She didn't mix the pound cake too much. Reece remembered reading somewhere that was bad.

By the time she pushed the cake into the warm oven, the cinnamon roll dough had risen. She punched it down and worked it again, then let it rise a second time.

The sugary aroma of the pound cake began to fill the kitchen. She searched the recipe book again until she found a recipe for brownies that were simple enough.

As she melted the butter, sugar and cocoa powder together, Reece felt in her bones that *this* was what she was meant to do. She wasn't supposed to walk the corridors of a massive hospital, being swallowed by the hundreds or thousands of other workers alongside her. She wasn't meant to diagnose. She was meant to create.

She popped the brownies into the oven as the side door opened. Chandler stepped in and inhaled. "Wow. That smells amazing." She spied her sister, her apron splattered with flour, and her eyes widened. "You okay?"

Reece grinned so hard her cheeks hurt. "Never better. Want to help?"

Chandler yawned. "No thanks. I'm too tired."

She deflated a little. It would've been nice to hang out with her sister some. They'd spent moments with their mother, but the girls hadn't had any one-on-one time besides what they spent in their room together.

She told her good night, then realized that the cinnamon rolls were ready to roll out and fill.

And that was how she worked, for hours—starting one project as soon as another finished. By the time the sun began to peek over the sky, sending golden light washing over the coast, Reece was exhausted. Her shoulders ached from all the kneading, and her feet killed her from standing for so long.

But she was pleased with herself, impressed even, as she surveyed her accomplishments. Cinnamon rolls, freshly baked bread, moist brownies, and pound cake all sat in the display case that had been empty except for the day's dessert—Coca Cola cake.

Tired and famished, Reece snatched a cinnamon roll and decided to snatch a moment of sunrise before she fell onto her bed to grab a few hours' sleep.

She leaned in the doorframe, staring at the quiet of Sugar Cove. To her left were shops and farther out, beach houses on stilts, their windows dark. Up ahead sat the gas station and to her right were more houses.

The breeze ticked up, and her newly cut bangs tapped her forehead. Reece smiled at how different the fringe shaped her face, made her eyes stand out. She loved her new look.

All was right in the world.

She sighed as she took a bite of the cinnamon roll. The pastry was perfect. Brown on bottom, but soft on the inside. The simple glaze of confectioner's sugar had dried to sugary peaks, and Reece licked icing from her lips.

The sound of pounding footsteps caught her attention. She glanced over and spotted a man jogging. His silhouette fell under a lamp, and Reece saw a mop of golden hair and a hard jaw.

He glanced up and saw her, his eyes wide in surprise. He spotted her eating and smiled. It was wide and nice, and Reece felt something stir inside her.

"Morning," he said. "Looks like a great breakfast."

As he ran on by she replied, "It sure is."

She finished eating and cleaned up. As she passed her mother in the hallway, all Reece could think about was that man, and she wondered if she would see him again.

CHAPTER 20
Chandler

The day that she met Hudson, rain poured from the sky. The subways filled with water, and it spilled onto the tracks. The deluge was so high the trains shut down.

Chandler was a subway junkie. She took the train everywhere because it was cheaper than a cab.

But that morning, with water dripping down her back and into her eyes, she hailed a taxi. Her vision was fuzzy, and she didn't notice that across the street, a man had hailed the exact same cab. She didn't see him race over puddles that littered the asphalt, had no idea that he was running late for a meeting.

All she knew was that when they both jumped into the exact same vehicle and their eyes locked, she felt as if she'd known him all her life.

Hudson would later reveal the exact same sensation, but right then and there, they decided to share the cab.

She glanced demurely at her folded hands in her lap. What was this strange tingle that danced down her spine when their gazes met?

His warm chocolate-colored eyes welcomed her. In the twenty-minute ride, she found out his name, that he knew the history of half of the buildings that they passed and that he felt like home.

By the time Hudson exited the vehicle, he knew that her eyes reminded him of the clear Gulf Coast waters (he visited Tampa every year), that her golden hair was the color of wheat kissed by the sun, and that one day he would marry her (but she did not know this).

Their love flared quickly. Chandler shared every detail of her life with him, even the embarrassing things she did as a child—tripping and falling flat on her face while sliding into home during a softball game. To her horror, this occurred right in front of Reid Sykes, the boy she liked at the time.

He could beat that, though. He once cast a fishing line and instead of it landing in the water, it landed in the hair of his crush, Harper Pickens. Harper had started screaming in fright, and he never got to kiss her.

They spent lazy Sunday mornings reading the paper. Chandler sipped coffee that he made for her. She showed him sketches of her art, and he loved every one, proclaiming her the most brilliant artist he'd ever known. And she felt like it, too, when she was in his arms.

But all of that was a year ago. It was before her father dropped dead and even before her art started drying up. She didn't understand why. With him, she felt full, overflowing with love and happiness. Her art should follow.

She wanted to rack it up to laziness, being so comfortably cozy in love that she didn't have inspiration, but that wasn't it, either.

There simply wasn't anything inspiring her anymore—not in New York, and she doubted anywhere.

Her phone rang while she sat outside listening to the waves crashing against the beach. Her gaze darted to the phone she clutched in her hand.

It was him. He always called at nine o'clock so that they could chat before bedtime.

"Hey," she said softly, answering.

"Hey yourself," he said slowly. Usually his voice was flirty, but tonight it was heavier.

"Everything okay?"

He exhaled a gusty sigh. "No, it's not."

Her heart drummed against her rib cage. Had something happened? "Are your parents okay? Are you okay?"

"Yes, they're fine." He released another loud breath of air, and she could almost see him sitting in his recliner, staring at the brick walls of his loft condo. "Why didn't you tell me about the show? That you weren't in it?"

The world fell away, and Chandler felt like she might fall out the chair she sat in. Her lips quaked. Her voice shook when she said, "You said you wouldn't go."

"*I* didn't. My mother did. She hadn't been in years and wanted to see what your new work was like. She was appalled and frankly embarrassed when Sophie explained what had happened." Hurt infused his voice and made her heart ache. "Why didn't you tell me?"

"I couldn't," she said weakly. "I just...couldn't."

He exhaled a gusty sigh. "Something is clearly wrong, and I don't know what it is. But I'm beginning to think it's me."

Right then her heart sliced in two. How could she reveal that she was a failure? Hudson raked in millions for his law firm. He was a success and always would be. His entire family was packed tight with surgeons, respected artists, lawyers. They breathed success, while right now the only air she inhaled was the stale oxygen of failure.

"You gotta give me something here," he said quietly. "I won't pretend to know what it's like to lose a father, and I don't know the whole story about the show, but you can't hide. I want you to take the time you need, but pushing me away isn't giving me confidence about us."

Tears spilled from her cheeks. She opened her mouth, completely planning to explain, but all that squeaked out was, "Can you come here?"

She didn't want to see Hudson, but she couldn't *not* see him either. He was the light in her life, and right now, even though her inspiration had abandoned her, she needed his steady presence.

While she waited for his answer, all she could hear was blood rushing through her ears. It felt like forever before he finally said, "I'll be on the first flight out."

CHAPTER 21

Ginny

The second day of the restaurant being fully open was just as successful as the first. The early lunch service filled quickly. People told her they'd heard to arrive early if they wanted to get a plate. The second service turned out just as popular, and her heart was full.

Reece had stayed up all night baking. What on earth was going on with her? She'd been slower than the day before in terms of serving customers and cleaning up, but her attitude had been cheerful, so Ginny was happy.

It was a nice change from what Reece could often be like—grumpy, worried.

She got those characteristics from Jack.

After they cleaned up lunch and had prepped for the next day, Chandler said, "Hudson's coming."

Her heart immediately felt lighter. "That's wonderful. When?"

"Right now. I'm going to meet him at the airport. Can I take your car?"

"Yes, of course. And we can all go out to dinner after." She realized the lighthouse was too small for all of them to stay at and she immediately regretted not offering him the couch. But even if she had, deep down Ginny suspected that Hudson's proper upbringing would mean that he would kindly reject the offer of a couch, not wanting to encroach on the already compact quarters.

Her face must've been lined with worry because Chandler said, "Don't fuss over him. Hudson won't want it, and he's staying at a B&B in Port St. Joe."

She felt some comfort in that. Chandler wrapped a light cotton wrap over her thin shoulders, and Ginny saw how fragile she really was. Why hadn't she noticed before? But for the past months she'd been so stuck in her own grief over Jack's death that it had been impossible to notice much *other* than her own problems.

Well, her life was getting back on track now. She could afford to pour more attention on her daughters, because they deserved it.

"I'll be back soon," her oldest said with a kiss to her cheek.

She absently touched the warm spot on her face. "Be careful. See you soon. Oh, and I'll make reservations somewhere."

Reece had disappeared to nap, and Ginny retreated to her room. As soon as she sat on the bed with a cup of warm tea beside her and the latest Kristin Hannah book in her lap, her phone rang.

Farrah's name blinked across the screen. Hungry to talk to her best friend, she placed the book aside and quickly answered.

"I've got so much to tell," she immediately squealed.

She laughed. "Tell me everything."

For thirty minutes Ginny gushed about how successful the last two days of business had been, thanking Farrah for her brilliant idea to create meals from the cookbook and serve them. Every lunch service had filled up nicely, and she thanked her friend again.

"There's no need to thank me," Farrah told her. "You're a brilliant cook. For too long your talents have gone unrecognized."

"Oh, I don't know about that. But there is something else."

Her voice dripped with intrigue. "Do tell."

"There's this man—Aiden. Very frustrating type. I first met him, and he suggested I bid on the lighthouse. Pushed me into it, actually."

"It's his fault you're blissfully happy?" her friend teased.

"No, you know what I mean. But then I ran into him on the beach, and he left in a very snobby way, saying his name and then just walking off."

"Is he handsome?"

"No. Yes. Maybe," Ginny replied, exasperated. "Not that it matters, but he has the warmest eyes, and he looks like he just stepped right out of the ocean."

"So he's a god, then."

"No, stop being silly. But you won't believe what happened the last time we met."

"I'm thinking I may need popcorn for this," Farrah teased.

"Anyway." Ginny ignored the good-natured ribbing. "He told the girls that he used to be a treasure hunter, and he invited us onto his boat. And then another time, right before he left, the man said something about me being so lovely that he would hate to have ruined my life—or something like that."

"Sounds like someone's in love."

"I'm not in love."

"Not you. *Him.*"

"But that's not the worst of it."

"There's more?" Farrah cooed.

"Yes, and I told him I'd go on his boat. With the girls. And I think he said something about it being a date." The more she revealed, the more horrified she was by her actions. "I can't go on a date."

"And why not?" Her friend inhaled deeply. "Don't you deserve a little happiness?"

Hesitation laced her voice thickly. "I don't know."

"Ginny Rigby," Farrah said sharply, "I've kept my mouth shut a long time about Jack, but I'm going to tell you right now that you deserve to go out with that man. You may not remember this, but right after you got married, that man cut you down. Do you recall his birthday? You hadn't been married long, and you were so excited to be newlyweds and start your own home that you made him that beautiful lemon drizzle cake. You worked on it all day, and I remember how beautiful it was—a browned Bundt cake with that light glaze dripping down the top of it. It looked like absolute heaven. Everyone at the party was drooling over it." She paused and Ginny cringed, because she knew where this story was going. "When you presented the cake to Jack, do you recall what he said?"

She did, and the memory burned sharp and painful in her mind. "He said that if I ate it, it would be a moment on my lips and a lifetime on my hips."

"He said it in front of everyone," her friend recalled, her voice laced with anger. "Right then and there, I wished that you'd never married him." She quickly retreated, as if to take the sting out of her words. "Now, you have two beautiful daughters, and I'm certainly happy that they're here. But I remember thinking, in that moment, that Jack Rigby was a real piece of work to insult his brand-new wife like that, in public company. And then, as the years progressed and I watched him wear fancy silk suits while you were still shopping consignment, I became angry. Yes, I did. You deserved to marry a man who worshipped you. All Jack ever worshipped, I suppose besides God on Sunday mornings, was his image, what he portrayed to the world. He never laid a physical hand on you, but that man had you in a psychological stranglehold. To be honest, I wasn't surprised when you told me that he had a second family." Farrah laughed bitterly. "Of course he did. Jack only cared about himself, and he proved that when he kicked you out of *your* house." She exhaled a weary sigh. "So there. I'm sorry if I've offended you."

But Farrah hadn't offended Ginny. To her own surprise, she found tears streaming down her face. Everything that she had said had been right—all of it. Jack had treated her more like a shell of a person rather than anyone fully fleshed out. She wondered if Savannah felt the same, stowed in a corner for most of her relationship with the man, forced to take a back seat to Jack's real family, his real life.

But then again, he'd spent a lot of time out of town, on business. Perhaps Jack had ingratiated himself into a different community and people saw him as a doting father and husband.

After all, anyone can wear wedding rings and call themselves married.

A burst of anger flooded her chest, and Ginny dabbed her eyes with tissues she'd taken from a box by her bed. "No, everything you've said is exactly right. I just never wanted to admit it to myself while we were married."

"I think," her best friend said slowly, as if rolling the thought over in her mind, "that you should consider going out on that man's boat. What was his name again?"

"It's Aiden, and I don't know. It's too soon."

"Surely the girls are all for it. Especially after you told them what Jack did to you."

Guilt gnawed at her belly. She still hadn't confessed that to her daughters, but admitting it made her feel like a huge failure.

"Well, um, naturally, they were upset," she lied. "And sure, they want me to meet new men. But it's still a bit early."

"For whom?" When she didn't answer, Farrah sighed again. "You've taken the first step of truly living your life. You've gained your independence. Now it's time to reclaim your love life."

She scoffed. "Tell that to my love life." Wanting to steer Farrah away from the girls, she said, "I'm on the anger stage of grieving. I looked it up. I still have loneliness, turning upward. What's after that? Oh, the reconstruction period, along with acceptance and hope."

"Are you sure that you're on anger? To me it seems like you're already on the reconstruction part. You've leaped into a new life."

"Trust me, I'm still on anger." Ginny sipped her mint tea. It soothed her senses nearly as much as it calmed her mind. "But maybe when I reach loneliness, I'll call Aiden."

"Don't wait too long," Farrah warned in a light voice. "He may have moved on if you keep him hanging."

She sighed. "He is good-looking."

"I knew it." Farrah laughed. After the sound faded, she added, "I'm not trying to preach gloom and doom, but it's time you lived your life. You've been given a second chance. Take it and make your life shine."

For too long she had lived in Jack's shadow, doing what he wanted. She'd already taken several steps that showed she longed for independence. But was she ready to let someone into her heart?

Not that Aiden was looking for love. But she had lived in a love desert with Jack, and now was only just beginning to drink from the cup of life.

She finished up the call and opened the drawer in her nightstand. She had tucked Aiden's number inside. Ginny wasn't sure if she had hidden it in there so that Reece would forget about the boat (she had been very excited about the idea of an excursion) or so that she herself could forget about the number and the possibilities that were buried in the ink.

Ginny sighed and studied the numbers on the back of a business card. She flipped it over, staring at it, her stomach fluttering with possibility.

After a long moment she came to a decision about whether to call him. She picked her phone up off her chest, where she'd laid it after hanging up with Farrah.

As she held the cell in one hand, Ginny dropped the card back into her drawer and shut it tight.

CHAPTER 22

Chandler

A
s soon as she laid eyes on Hudson, Chandler immediately regretted her decision of asking him to come. He arrived with a leather duffel bag slung over his shoulder, his tweed blazer over a light blue shirt. He beamed when he saw her, and as they approached one another outside of the gate, the rest of the world melted into the background.

Hudson stared down at her with eyes full of warmth and love. "Hey, gorgeous."

He brushed his lips over hers, and she felt a tingle dance down her spine. "Hey, handsome."

It was their normal greeting and it felt right, but at the same time so wrong, for she immediately felt selfish calling him to her.

He would want answers, an explanation of *why* she was being so cold, and Chandler wasn't sure if she was ready to admit the truth.

It was easier explaining this to her family because they had known her before she was a success. But not him. He'd known her when her art was growing, when her abilities were expanding instead of shrinking.

He threaded his fingers through hers, and as they walked, Hudson's shoulders brushed hers. Every once in a while, she would get a whiff of his scent. Hudson smelled of leather and cedar. The smell wrapped itself around Chandler, and she pressed her body closer to his.

He asked her how her mom was, and she told him about the restaurant's success. He talked animatedly about a new client he'd just won, and though he dreaded the load of work it would bring, he said that this would help secure future dealings.

She felt his gaze on her then, warm and bright, when he talked about the future. Chandler murmured how proud she was of him, and then he sank back onto the seat of the car, watching the scenery fly by.

For a late lunch they stopped by Killer Seafood in Mexico Beach. They sat outside at one of the long tables as they waited for their servings of Killer Simmerin' Sauce with shrimp and scallops served in bread bowls. The restaurant had been a freestanding building before the hurricane hit. Now the kitchen was in a food truck across the street from the beach.

Hudson grabbed the food when it was ready, and she inhaled the savory red sauce. It smelled of shrimp and tomatoes. It tasted even better than it looked.

He ate a spoonful and nodded. "Delicious, but I can't wait to try your mom's food tomorrow. She's a great cook."

"Thanks." She looked up, suddenly realizing that eating out might've been a mistake. "We could've waited to eat."

"First of all," he said, giving her a wry smile, "I wanted you all to myself for a few minutes before I saw the rest of your family. Last time I met Reece, she bombarded me with questions about my family and my job."

She quirked a brow, thinking about how her sister had pounced on that Aiden guy. "You'll be happy to know that she hasn't changed."

"I bet not." He held her gaze until she felt the weight of his unsaid question bearing down on her. Her eyes cut back to her soup. "What's going on? What aren't you telling me?"

She twisted her napkin between her fingers. Not wanting to lie, she skirted the truth. "I didn't think that I would ever want to leave New York, you know? But I really like it here."

His gaze followed hers to the beach. The sun was low in the sky, and they could just see the tops of the waves as they broke on the sand.

"It's beautiful," he confirmed, though his eyes narrowed in confusion. He shifted on the seat, obviously uncomfortable. "But your life is in New York."

"I know," she murmured.

"This is a great place to take a break, so take one." He forced a tight smile, and she did the same. "But everything you've built is in the city."

"Right. I know."

"And I was hoping..."

Her gaze latched to on to his. "Hoping what?"

"That someday our lives will join." He paused as if waiting for his words to sink in, but she shoved them far into the corners of her mind, not wanting to process one idea when she hadn't even fixed her main problem yet. "But my work isn't here. My family, my job is in New York."

His jaw was set firmly, and she nodded. "I know."

He dropped his plastic spoon into the bread bowl and slid his hand over the picnic table. Hudson took her hand and entwined her fingers with his.

"If it's your dad, I understand. There's no rule book for grieving."

"That's not it."

"Then what is it? Please tell me." His gaze searched her, and when she didn't answer, he dropped her hand and shifted away. His gaze cut to the ocean. Golden sunlight broke across his skin, and the wind lifted his wavy hair, which had curled in the Florida humidity. "I'm beginning to think this is about me. That you're avoiding me for some reason. You've been distant. Sometimes I have to pull conversation from you. You're different."

The pain etched in his eyes killed her. She couldn't let him believe that he was the cause of her problems. She dropped her face in her hands and told him everything—about Sophie kicking her out of the show, how she lacked a muse, inspiration.

Hudson listened quietly, the worry in his eyes slowly fading as he realized that he wasn't the reason behind her suffering. When she'd finished telling him everything, he sat for a minute.

They were finished eating, and he dumped their Styrofoam plates in the trash and then took her hand and headed to the beach. They walked across the sand packed hard from the pounding of the waves. Sandpipers scuttled across the surface in search of food, and the sound of the water calmed her pounding heart.

"This is normal. You lost your dad. Of course you can't create," he told her as he ran his fingers over the back of her hand.

She shook her head. "You don't understand. This was happening before my dad died. I created those pieces for Sophie months ago. It's gone, Hudson. It's all gone. I don't have any more to create inside of me. I'm empty."

"It's okay; we'll get through it together."

Those words should have been calming, but for some reason they only made her feel worse. "I can't be the failure in your life."

He squinted, which made his beautiful features harden. "What are you talking about?"

"Your family is successful. You're on top of the world. How can I compete with that?"

"Compete? Our relationship isn't about competing. What are you talking about?"

She tugged her hand from his and balled up her fists. "No one in your family is a failure. What would I be, the pitiful artist girlfriend who was successful for a New York minute and then burst into flames? I can't handle that kind of pressure."

"No one's putting that on you," he argued, "but yourself."

He didn't get it. Hudson simply didn't understand. "Next to you, I'm a failure. And who will you be beside me? Someone who pities a fallen artist. I can't take that. I don't want your pity."

He took a step back and studied Chandler as if really seeing her for the first time. "Do you think I'm that shallow?"

When she didn't answer, he punched his hands into his pockets. His jaw jumped as he turned to watch the waves.

Her stomach was clenched tight. "I know that you're not shallow. That's not it. But what I'm saying is the truth. I can't be a failure, and that's all I would be."

He rocked back onto his heels as he took in what she was saying. It felt like a great boulder had been removed from her gut. *Finally*. She'd told him. The words were out there. She couldn't take them back.

When Hudson spoke, sorrow filled his voice. "I don't ever want you to feel like a failure. You're not to me. But if by being with me, you feel that way, well, I can't stop that."

Chandler parted her lips to speak, but her teeth chattered. She suddenly felt cold, so very cold, as if her frosty words had stolen all the warmth from her body.

He watched her carefully. It was impossible to read him. His face was a stony mask. After a few moments he pointed to the car.

"We'd better go say hello to your mom and sister."

She followed him off the beach, wondering if she'd just made the worst mistake of her life.

* * *

At dinner Hudson was perfect. He made everyone laugh with stories of how as a child, he was convinced that mermaids lived in the Florida waters.

Everyone laughed but her. She forced herself to smile, but that was the most she could manage. She simply felt hollowed out, her life scooped from her.

After dinner she drove Hudson to the bed-and-breakfast he was staying at. She walked him to the front steps, and he leaned in and kissed her cheek.

She drank in his scent, and it took everything she had not to curl her fingers into his shirt and let him drag her inside. But she knew that if she did that, there would be no going back. She would be lost in him. Though part of her wanted the security that his steadfast presence always offered, the other half of her didn't. She needed to be alone.

He told her good night, and then he disappeared behind the door. She walked back to the car with tears spilling from her eyes.

The next morning he called early and said that he was leaving that afternoon. "My plane departs at one. That gives me time to have lunch at the Lighthouse Café."

"I can drive you to the airport," she lied. Taking him would put her mother in a lurch. She needed the extra help to get through the second lunch service.

"No, it's okay. I'll call an Uber. I'll be there at eleven."

When they hung up, she felt like the very last part of her insides were being scraped out. But she could only be angry at herself because she knew this was the way things would go. She couldn't break Hudson's heart and not also break her own.

And her heart was breaking for losing what they'd had. He might not understand why she was doing this, but it was for the best.

The morning whisked by. Before she knew it, it was eleven and Hudson was strolling into the restaurant. Her mother was serving him beef in red wine sauce, and he was chewing and smiling.

She caught him looking at her once, and the pain in his eyes made her feel like a barb was ripping through her heart. Chandler inhaled a shaky breath and walked over to speak to him, but he was detached, distant.

Later they said goodbye on the beach. He gave her a tight hug and kissed the top of her head. "Take care. I'll let you know when I land safely."

"Thank you," she said.

Then his Uber arrived, and she burned to tell him more, to take back everything that she'd said, that she didn't want to break up. But Chandler knew in her heart this was the right thing.

For Hudson.

In time he would see that. He would understand that this had been the right choice.

The only question that remained was, would she ever see it that way? Or would the hole that was already opening in her chest, the one created by his absence, grow bigger until it swallowed her up?

CHAPTER 23

Reece

Every afternoon Reece napped, and every morning she awoke at two a.m. to bake.

She poured over the old cookbook and made chocolate drop cookies filled with coconut and pecans. She made chess and lemon pies, German chocolate cake and light-as-air divinity.

She saw it as her nightly duty to create the sweets from the book. Her mother liked focusing on the first and second courses for the café's menu, so it was easy convincing her mother to allow her the chance at creating the desserts.

Every morning the pie and cake cases were full, and by the afternoon they were sold out, all the sweets eaten by happy customers.

But at the break of dawn, hours before a single dessert ever touched a customer's lips, Reece would stand in the open doorway of the lighthouse, snacking on bread or cake, or sometimes just toast. It was during those yawning hours that the man would run by.

At first she was shy, just waving every now and then. But once he said when running (his eyes the most startling shade of ocean blue), "I was wondering when you were going to tempt me with dessert."

She laughed. "You're welcome to one."

"That's okay." He smiled, showing off his dimples. "I'd rather smell whatever it is you're baking. What'd you make today?"

"Tea cakes."

"Smells delicious."

And that was how it went. Reece baked until dawn, and then she'd drink her coffee and chat with the runner every morning, wondering what his name was and wondering if he wondered what hers was.

She wasn't telling hers until he asked. That was how she had been brought up, and that was how it would go. But she did so desperately want to know his name.

But he hadn't revealed it in the several weeks that he'd gone by, and as time passed it became an uncomfortable lump in her throat. It was as if the window of opportunity, the one where you introduced yourself had slipped away, and so they were stuck in an uneasy limbo. It was too late to ask his name (not that she would), and it was too late for him to ask hers.

At this point it seemed rude to ask anyway. If he'd wanted her name, he would've already asked it. So that meant he wasn't interested in her.

The thought made her shoulders sag as she sipped her early morning coffee. The bread was baking, and the smell of yeast filled the room. It was too early for her gentleman caller to, um, *not* call on her.

Reece, being bored and tired of the small lighthouse, decided to head across the street to the grocery store. Maybe she'd eat something savory for breakfast.

The inside of the store smelled of cooked sausage and biscuits. Her stomach growled at the delightful mingling of aromas.

"How're y'all?" Shelby said from behind the cash register.

She shot her friend a warm smile. "We're all good. How're y'all?"

"Doing well. Just living it up in the gas station." Reece laughed at her joke, and Shelby leaned over the counter, her eyes gleaming with intrigue. "But what I want to know is—what're you baking today? I can't smell it, but it looks good on you."

She glanced down at her flour-drenched apron. Embarrassed, she wiped some of the flour away, but that just smeared it.

"Some fresh bread," she admitted.

"Mm hm. Sounds delicious. You are gonna capture the best man in Sugar Cove with your baking abilities."

Reece winced. "I don't know about that. I don't have time to meet anybody."

Which was completely true. Baking and serving customers left little room for pesky things such as flirting with men who were not quite strangers and answering the emails from her advisor at Tulane that were piling up in her inbox.

Shelby pulled her strawberry-blonde hair over one shoulder and began braiding it. "Why don't you come out with me this Friday? I'm meeting up with some friends and you can tell me what you think about my secret crush."

Her brows lifted at that. "Secret crush? I'd almost forgotten. You mean that man hasn't asked you out yet?"

Shelby's pale cheeks turned a rosy shade. "He doesn't know that I'm alive, but I don't care. Come meet him. Get out of that stuffy old lighthouse for one night."

"Well," she hesitated.

"If Reece wants to live her life in a stuffy old lighthouse, you should let her," Vera said, shuffling behind the breakfast counter.

Shelby rolled her eyes at her grandmother's intrusion. "It's a beautiful lighthouse, but you're too young to trap yourself in a tower and waste away for a fisherman that will crash against the rocks."

"You talking about ghost stories?" Vera huffed.

She flashed her grandmother a wide grin. "Only the good ones."

Reece glanced out the window. The moon hung high in the sky, bathing the ocean in its light. Its beams poured over the tower, making the white building almost seem to glow ethereally. From this distance, she understood why Shelby referred to the place as something to be trapped in. Because it looked like a formidable prison that could house a princess. But to her, the lighthouse wasn't a prison. It was her salvation. Because she felt herself opening like a flower, blooming, even though her poor sister was wilting.

Things had seemed tense between Chandler and Hudson, but Chandler had offered no explanation and Reece didn't press her.

Maybe it would be best if they both went out.

"Can my sister come, too?" she asked Shelby.

Her friend brightened. "Of course."

They made plans to chat later in the week. The sun was about to break across the horizon and Reece was still starving, so she ordered a sausage biscuit. Vera wrapped it in paper and Reece smiled to herself as she made her way back to the café.

She spotted the man running down the road. She was a little way off and considered calling out but decided against it.

But her heart ballooned when he paused for a moment outside the lighthouse. He looked inside but saw only an empty dining room. Then he continued on, and she smiled to herself.

Oh yes, he was interested in her, at least as a friend. That was all the sign she needed to give her hope, because what often started out as friendship could blossom into more.

Couldn't it?

CHAPTER 24

Ginny

Aiden ate at the restaurant three days that week. She always had a warm smile for him, and he seemed to have the same for her, too. They chatted easily enough whenever she refilled his iced tea and asked how the food was. He always complimented her cooking and she thanked him. He didn't push about going on his boat, and for that she was glad.

Her life, without her even realizing it, had slipped into a smooth routine. She awoke every morning to greet the day. The view from her bedroom window was breathtakingly gorgeous. Looking out at the breaking waves and sun-kissed sand filled her heart with joy.

But for as happy as she was, Ginny watched Chandler sink into a gloomy solitude. Ever since Hudson had left, her oldest daughter had been quiet, shying away from spending time with them. No matter how hard Ginny tried to lull her from this sadness with trips shopping or going out to eat, she refused.

It was as if because her daughter was artistically broken, that she couldn't imagine pulling herself from that mire. She continued to sink deeper.

Ginny had the perfect solution. She would call Aiden and take him up on his offer for a boat ride. The fresh salty air and bouncing on the waves could warm Chandler's chilled heart.

But just as she was about to call him, her phone rang. It was Farrah.

"Hey," she said happily. "How're you?"

"Let's not talk about me. Whatever you're doing right now, I need you to drop it."

She laughed nervously. "Okay, but why?"

"I looked up that Aiden fellow and called him. Before you tell me that I shouldn't have, I know you. You never would've done it. So I did it for you. He's taking you and the girls out on his boat today."

"What did you say?" Ginny dropped her face in her hands. "I'm so embarrassed. And for your information, I was just about to call him myself."

"First of all," Farrah said sternly, "he was so charmed that I called for you. I simply explained that you'd never call and that you would love to go. He thought it was sweet."

"More like psychopathic that I'd have a friend call for me."

"I told him that you didn't know what I was doing."

"I'm sure he believed you," she said sarcastically.

"Ginny Rigby, you're too old to worry about silly matters like that. Besides, don't you want to know what he said?"

She did want to know. Putting her embarrassment aside, she said, "What did he say?"

"That he would love to take you and the girls out. He'd been waiting to hear from you."

Her heart ping-ponged in her chest. "He said that?"

"Mm hmm," Farrah told her. "And you're lucky that I'm happily married because he has the sexiest voice. I almost want to book a flight down just to see him."

"Stop."

"Now hurry. Let me give you the address to the marina and the directions."

She jotted everything down and happened to catch a glimpse of herself in the mirror. Oh goodness. Her hair was tied back into a frizz ball. She needed to smooth it out and apply some makeup. And change her clothes. There was so much to do before heading out.

Not that it was a date, or anything.

She hung up after promising to call with all the juicy details (not that there would be any). Then she quickly called the girls from the back room and told them to get ready.

The three of them had a date with a treasure hunter.

* * *

Aiden was already on his boat when they arrived. Reece practically bounded down the wooden walkway, rushing to him.

Chandler slunk behind, her entire mood shrouded in sorrow. Ginny smiled at her oldest. "We won't be gone long."

She nodded absently as they strolled up to the boat. Aiden beamed down at them with a relaxed, friendly smile. He wore khaki shorts and boat shoes, along with a linen button-down shirt with the sleeves rolled up, revealing muscular forearms.

"Just in time." He offered his hand to Ginny. She slid her palm over his and felt an immediate spark on her skin. Heat crept up her cheeks, and she glanced shyly away, silently scolding herself for being so juvenile.

She was a fifty-year-old woman, for goodness' sake. Not a teenager.

"Thank you for coming," he said.

"Thank you for offering."

Amusement sparkled in his eyes. "But it wasn't you who called me."

"You caught me."

He winked at her and then helped Chandler aboard. Reece was already staking claim to a seat up front.

"Welcome, ladies," he said. "We're not going to go out too far, but far enough that maybe we can see a school of dolphins up close and personal."

"What about fishing?" Reece asked.

"Gotta have a license," he said to a disappointed Reece. He noted her disappointment and added, "But tell you what—before you come out next time, I'll get you set up with a license and then we can do some fishing."

"Sounds great."

He nodded to a picnic basket settled in the front of the boat, beneath two seats. "There are also snacks if you get hungry."

Ginny suspected that he was quite pleased to be taking them out, so she teasingly said, "What kind of snacks?"

"Oh, nothing much. Just a few things I picked up."

But her youngest already had the lid open. "There's fried chicken and boiled eggs. There's even potato salad in individual cups."

"Just a few things, huh?" Ginny said.

He smiled bashfully. "I know someone who caters. I can't take several ladies on my boat without offering refreshments." He turned to the girls. "Now. Is everyone ready?"

"Sure are," Reece said loudly.

Chandler only nodded and Ginny deflated a little, wishing that her daughter would at least try to have fun. But she didn't know what it was like to lose a muse, so she was unsure how to console her oldest.

Reece helped Aiden unmoor the boat, and the women took seats while the craft glided away from the marina on the bay into the emerald waters of the Atlantic.

Chandler sat in the bow with her sister, and both girls leaned back, lifting their chins to the sun as it slowly sank in the horizon.

Ginny felt wrong just sitting while their host steered them out into the ocean, so she moved to stand beside him at the helm.

"What a glorious view," she said, pointing to the horizon.

He dragged his gaze from the ocean to her. "It sure is."

Right then, Reece turned around. "Dolphins!"

She pointed off in the distance, and Ginny spotted three dolphins leaping into the water. Aiden slowed the boat. "I'll cut the engine in a minute, and we'll slowly slide up to them."

They did so and the dolphins saw them, bobbing up and down in the water as if waiting for them to arrive. She held her breath, figuring that the creatures would swim off, but the dolphins stayed, their slick skin glistening in the sunlight.

"Oh my gosh," Reece chirped. "They're letting us get so close."

"I think they want to ride the wake," he said.

She wrinkled her nose. "What's that?"

"When I take off, it makes it easier for them to swim. They don't have to work as hard. Want to see if I'm right?"

"Yes."

"Okay, y'all. Get ready. We're about to take off." He turned to Ginny. "You want to sit?"

"No, I'll stay here if that's okay."

"Fine by me."

He started the boat and slowly pulled away from the dolphins, which followed. As he increased the speed, the dolphins matched it, jumping and swimming to everyone's delight. The creatures seemed to smile and enjoy riding in the boat's wake as much as Ginny loved watching it.

Reece had her phone out and was videoing the entire event while Chandler glanced over her shoulder, a thin smile on her lips.

A small smile was better than none.

After a few minutes the dolphins swam away, and he slowed the boat.

Reece beamed at him. "That was so fun."

"They rode with us a long time," he murmured.

She clapped her hands. "You've got to tell us about treasure hunting!"

"I will," he called back.

"You've got quite a fan club in her," she joked.

"Just her?"

Her chest fluttered with nerves. She smiled at him, unsure exactly how to flirt back. It had been too long since she'd attempted to make this sort of small talk with anyone.

But she was saved when he stopped the boat after they'd sailed out a little farther. "Time to show y'all how to treasure hunt."

Reece popped up from her seat. "Really?"

He smiled. "Really."

She watched while he opened a compartment and pulled out a long rope with what looked like a large metal hockey puck at the end.

Aiden spoke as he unwound the rope. "My dad was a fisherman. When he wasn't using his boat, he let me borrow it to treasure hunt. Mostly I just found small things—bracelets, rings. But one day I struck it big."

Reece's eyes widened and Ginny couldn't help but delight in the wonder brimming in her youngest's eyes. Chandler had come over, too, and she peered at him with a reserved curiosity.

"How'd you strike it big?" Reece asked.

He swung the metal puck in a loop several times before tossing it into the ocean. "It's well-known in these parts that lots of Spanish ships were lost in storms, sinking to the bottom of the ocean and taking with them, gold."

"And you found the gold?" she asked.

He nodded. "I was lucky, and the weather was just right. So yes, I found it and that started my journey."

Chandler wrinkled her nose. "Is that all you found?"

If Aiden was put off by her attitude, he didn't show it. He simply nodded. "My name got out and other people hired me to help them find treasure. But I always hunt for myself."

He handed the rope to Reece. "Pull it in and see what you've got."

She stared at it in confusion. "Pull what in?"

He nodded to the ocean. "That metal disc I tossed in was a magnet. Let's see what you can find."

She squealed before tugging the rope. "It's heavy."

"It has to be. That's how you find real treasure."

There wasn't anything on the end of the magnet, but they tossed it out a few more times and were able to recover, to Reece's glee, a gold earring.

"How cool! Want to try, Chandler?"

"No, I need to use the ladies' room."

He gestured to the steps that led to the cabins below. "Right that way."

She thanked him and disappeared. Reece continued to toss out the puck, clearly bitten by the treasure-hunting bug.

Ginny leaned over . "Thank you again for bringing us out."

He nodded as he watched Reece tug on the line. "I had a feeling it might be good for y'all."

"What would make you say that?"

His blue eyes locked onto her. "What would make a stranger buy a lighthouse on a whim?"

She scoffed. "If you remember correctly, I was goaded."

"By me?" He shook his head. "I don't think so. When I saw you, I recognized something in you that I've seen before in myself."

"And that is?" she asked, doubtful that he had any idea of what lay in her heart.

"Betrayal and pain," he said quietly so that her daughter wouldn't hear.

A stab of agony pierced her heart. She dropped her head and nodded. "It was a crazy day before. My life got completely turned upside down." She nodded to her daughter. "Neither of them knows that, though."

His gaze slid back to the ocean. "Divorce will do that to a person. It took a long time for my ex and I to become friends."

"I only wish things were so easy for me." Ginny flexed her fingers. She had pent-up energy that she didn't know what to do with. "My husband died and left me with a surprise."

He shifted toward her, turning his body in her direction, and with the movement Aiden's salt and spicy scent trickled up her nose. "I'd love to hear it over dinner."

She laughed nervously. "I don't know."

"No pressure," he told her. "Just as friends. I could always use a friend."

She glanced shyly at him and saw genuine warmth in his eyes. Her heart softened a bit.

Then she remembered something. "Why were you there, at the auction that day? And why did you let me win?"

He chuckled. "Correction—I didn't *let* you win. You outbid me. And as for what I was doing there—"

Reece pointed out. "More dolphins!"

She leaned over the starboard side, and sure enough, sailing through the air before sliding back into the water, swam a family of dolphins.

The school swam past, splashing water each time they glided into the ocean. Ginny wished Chandler was up here to watch this. Surely this would cheer her heart.

As the dolphins swam away, she turned her attention back to Aiden. He watched the water with a genuine fondness that she found charming, even intriguing.

"You love the ocean," she remarked.

"I do." He dragged his eyes once again from the water, as if it was the hardest thing on earth for him to do. But when his gaze landed on her, she felt a giddy nervousness singing in her bones.

It was an emotion that she didn't know how to process, so she returned to their previous conversation.

"You were saying why you were at the auction?" she prodded.

He scrubbed a hand down his jaw. "I was there because my grandfather used to be the keeper of the lighthouse. When I was a kid, I would visit him and climb those stairs until my legs ached. It holds good memories," he told her, his eyes full of wistfulness.

Ginny suddenly felt guilty for having outbid him. "Oh," was all she could say.

He touched her shoulder then, softly, like she might break. "It wasn't mine to have. If it makes you feel better, that's how I see it. It's yours and I couldn't be happier for you."

"Maybe we should go home," Reece said sharply, dropping the seaweed-drenched magnet onto the deck. She stared openly at Aiden's hand perched on her shoulder. Ginny suddenly felt very conspicuous as little pinpricks of unease danced up and down her spine.

He slowly pulled back his hand, but his fingers trailed down the back of her arm, lighting her skin on fire. "Sure thing. I'll turn around right now."

CHAPTER 25
Chandler

She didn't know what all the fuss was about on deck, but Chandler didn't care.

She'd come downstairs to use the bathroom and had discovered more than she ever bargained for.

One wall of the lower deck was painted a pale gray and a glass case was attached to it. It wasn't the case itself that stole her breath, it was what was behind the glass.

Glued to a black backing were dozens of seashells. But these weren't ordinary broken shells. These gleamed as if they'd been made from mother-of-pearl and dropped straight into the churning waters of the ocean. They were all labeled, and she traced her finger over the glass, murmuring their names.

"Lightning whelk," she said in awe, admiring the spiral of its top.

The pale orange of the Florida fighting conch reminded her of the sun when it rose. It also reminded her of a pale garnet.

The shark-eye moon was an iridescent gray shell that spiraled out in beautiful swirls.

And there were more. A spotted junonia was beautiful to behold with its smooth surface and delicate opening.

How had Chandler missed all of this? She'd been at the beach for weeks, sulking in her own unhappiness. What was wrong with her? She'd pulled herself out of the quagmire before. She'd built her brand from the ground up.

Yes, she'd lost her muse, but she could reclaim it.

She was reclaiming it. Right now.

She flexed her fingers, itching to grab a sketchpad and start working. There was so much here, so many shells, so much beauty.

She pulled out her phone and snapped a quick picture. Her mind was already churning with ideas, possibilities. So many thoughts spilled over in her head that she couldn't wait to return home.

Chandler raced back on deck. The boat's nose was aimed for the shore, and Reece sat with her shoulders straight.

She made eye contact with her sister, and Reece slid her eyes toward their mother and Aiden.

Chandler didn't care if her mother liked Aiden. Their father was gone, and her mother didn't need to be alone. She deserved to live.

Her sister needed to calm down. After all, it wasn't like her mother was about to get married.

But Chandler had other things to focus on. Right now her muse was firing on all cylinders.

She couldn't wait to start creating.

There was only one problem. She didn't have any of her smithing tools in Florida with her.

Hudson would ship them to her. Her stomach tightened at the thought. She couldn't ask him. Not after how she'd left things.

Then an idea sparked in her mind. It was crazy and a little off the wall. But could she...? Would it...?

It was just so crazy that it just might work.

CHAPTER 26

Ginny

"We've got a profit," she exclaimed the next day. Ginny pointed to a laptop, which was open with a wide spreadsheet on it, and threw up her hands. "Girls! We're in the black!"

Reece left the sink full of dishes to come see, and Chandler drifted in from the dining room holding a broom.

Her youngest peeked at the screen. "Let me look."

Ginny splayed her hands, a smile so wide on her face that her cheeks hurt. "Look right there, that last line. After three weeks of sold-out lunches, we're making a profit."

"All thanks to Grandma's cookbook," Chandler added.

She gave both her daughters a pointed look. "And with a little help from y'all. I owe so much to you both, but I completely understand if you want to go back to your lives. Reece, maybe you can pick up next semester at Tulane and not be so far behind."

Her gaze darted to the floor. "Yeah, maybe."

"Don't you want to go back, honey?"

"Yeah," she replied a little too loudly. "Of course. But there's summer school, like I told you."

The look of trouble in her eyes made Ginny's stomach tighten. Her daughter was holding something back.

"But anyway," Reece said with a gusty sigh, "I've got plans tonight."

Her brows perked up at that. "Oh? You don't want to celebrate with me?"

"No. Nah." She kissed her cheek. "I'd love to, but I'm already busy. Chandler's invited, too."

Chandler stopped sweeping and glanced at her sister in surprise. "I'm invited where?"

"*Out.* Some of us are going out if you want to come."

She shook her head, and Reece's beaming face withered. To soften the blow Ginny said, "We can always celebrate tomorrow. Unless Chandler planned to surprise me by spending the evening with me?"

She shook her head. "No, I've got...other things going on."

But what other things?

Her girls were such mysteries. It was obvious to her that they were keeping secrets. But Ginny couldn't point fingers because she still hadn't told them about Jack's betrayal.

She would.

It would happen.

One day.

And that voice of his, which whispered in her ear at the worst times, was slowly fading into the background. Ginny inhaled deeply and felt pride in what she had accomplished in a short time.

There was enough money in the bank to keep the business open and to feed and clothe herself. In her opinion, that meant she was a success.

The girls went back to work, and she considered her plight for a moment. She could spend a cozy night at home reading, or she could celebrate with someone.

She pulled her wallet from her purse and eyed two business cards—one for her old sorority sister Molly, and the other belonged to Aiden.

She felt a swell of happiness in her chest just thinking of the boat trip that Aiden had taken them on. But she hadn't seen Molly since she'd eaten lunch at the opening of the Lighthouse Café.

After considering both people for a moment, she made her decision. Then she pulled her phone from her purse, retreated to her room while the girls finished cleaning, and dialed the number.

CHAPTER 27

Reece

"Why don't you ever want to spend time with me?"

She stood in their shared bedroom, staring at her sister, who was deep into reading a sheet of paper that she had spread over a notepad. Was that a letter?

Chandler dragged her gaze from the page and focused on her, a frown line deepening between her brows. "What are you talking about?"

Reece felt courageous. Baking these past weeks had given her purpose. Seeing the expressions of delight on customer's faces had breathed life into her soul.

It gave her enough strength to tackle this conversation with her sister. "Why aren't you coming out tonight?"

"There's just something I need to do, is all."

"What?"

She shrugged. "It's nothing big."

"Then why can't you tell me?"

She made her way over to the bed and sat, feeling the mattress sag beneath her. Chandler and Reece had never shared a bedroom, not the whole time that they were growing up. They'd always had separate spaces, and even though they were technically living in the same space now, the emotional distance between them might as well have been as wide as the Grand Canyon for as much as they really knew one another.

Chandler shook her head. "Because I'm not ready to share it, okay? I'm not like you. I don't have to tell everybody everything all the time."

Those words bit into her heart. "I don't tell everybody everything."

Her sister dipped her head in a way that said, *Yes, you do.* "Really. As soon as I came up from below Aiden's deck, I knew that you were ticked about something that happened between him and Mama."

She scoffed. "He touched her arm."

"And that's a problem, why?"

Reece threw her hand toward the door. "Do I have to remind you that our father just died?"

"Of course not. I was there. But if she wants to see this guy, let her. It's not as if Dad was the best husband in the world."

She felt a second punch to the gut. "What do you mean?"

Chandler folded up the sheet of paper and slipped it into her purse. "Can you really tell me that you never noticed how her clothes always came from consignment but his and ours never did? How Mama scraped away pennies while he played golf at the club? How he persuaded you into medical school even though you didn't want to?"

It felt like her heart was being sliced in two. She would not let her sister win this conversation. There went her sister, being holier than thou. Well, she wasn't going to have any of it.

"Of course I wanted to go to medical school."

"Then why aren't you there?"

"Because I'm grieving, thank you very much. And so is our mother."

You'll never be the beauty that your sister will be, Reece. You've got to have something else to fall back on.

Pain ripped through her heart as she heard her father's voice bellowing in her head.

Chandler sighed in that delicate way of hers, that way that she never could master. She was all grace and beauty, whereas Reece was spunk and cuteness.

Her sister rose from the bed and smiled sympathetically. "You may have Mama fooled, that you love what you're doing, but I know you."

That burned her up. "How could you know me when you never spend time with me?"

Her eyes became big as plates. "What are we doing? We're living in the same room. I see you every day. I work with you every morning. I'm spending almost every waking minute with you."

But they weren't minutes that counted. They were work and not quality time. She felt her inside withering, her voice thinning. Her sister didn't understand how much Reece wanted them to be best friends. She was too wrapped up in her own misery to see anything else.

Her sister was a lost cause. She waved her hand in dismissal. "You're right. I don't know what I'm talking about."

Chandler nodded, seeming satisfied with her answer, though Reece's heart shrank. "I suggest you tell Mama sooner rather than later about medical school."

"Tell her what?"

Chandler pulled her hair into a ponytail and secured it. She checked her reflection in the mirror, and Reece tried not to be jealous of her flawless skin, the sprinkling of adorable freckles across her nose, the blue eyes like sapphires.

"Tell Mama that you're not going back to Tulane. That's what. The longer you drag it out, the harder it's going to be to explain."

Without another word, she left the room, leaving in her wake the faint smell of lilies.

Reece felt like her insides had been scooped out. Her sister was right. She didn't want to return to Tulane—ever.

Perhaps Chandler knew her better than she realized.

CHAPTER 28

Chandler

Hudson was writing her letters, letters that made her throat shrivel from guilt. She'd barely had time to tuck the last one away before Reece spied it and started asking questions.

Reece. How could she think they didn't spend time together? They were in each other's company all day, every day. No, she didn't share her deepest thoughts because her sister wouldn't understand. Her life had been picked out for her. School came easy. She'd received straight A's since first grade and sailed all the way through high school and college, blowing away the MCAT, the exam for entry into medical school. Brilliant Reece, who could master any skill with ease.

You're the pretty one, Chandler, her father had said. *Your looks will get you by.*

She curled her fingers into white-knuckled fists. She wanted to be more than simply a beautiful face, and she had been until now.

She'd called an Uber, which took her to downtown Port St. Joe. She found a bench and sat, wanting to finish the letter that Hudson had written. Reece had walked into the room before she'd had a chance to get very far in it.

She pulled the heavy stock paper from her purse and unfolded it on her lap before smoothing the page.

He had written the letter by hand in dark blue ink. Somehow that made her heart break even more.

. . .

Chandler,

It's taken me time to know how to write this letter. There is so much to say. For days after I returned to New York, I was angry—at myself for not knowing how to convince you that you are all I need in this world. There is nothing and no one else that makes me a better person the way that you do.

Seeing you smile is like watching the sun rise—it is truly an awesome thing to witness, and for me to know how much you're suffering and that you want to do it alone kills me.

I'm not going to try to convince you to call me or come back to me.

But know that I'll be waiting. When you're ready to talk to me, I'll answer on the first ring.

With all my heart and love,
Hudson

She didn't know which crushed her heart more—that he would wait for her or that he'd written the letter.

Both made her heart ache. So many times her finger had hovered over his name on her phone, and every time, she pulled her thumb away.

She couldn't be with him until she righted this within herself. It wasn't fair. Hudson's family was all prestige, and if she couldn't bring that to the table, then she would never feel adequate.

Across the street, a door opened, and Chandler's gaze darted up. She glanced at her watch. It was nearly five o'clock. The last customer had left the jewelry store. Now it was time for her to make her move.

She rose, her stomach a whirlwind of knots. She had one shot at this and one shot only. In that instant she regretted not having brought the box of cast-off jewelry with her. She should have. But it was too late now. Her feet were quickly moving her across the street toward the door.

A bell ding-donged as she entered. A wall of cool air rushed over her, making goose bumps ripple across her skin.

From behind a jewelry counter a woman wearing a bright sea-blue and watermelon-pink kaftan glanced up and smiled. She wore the most exquisite jewelry—a turquoise teardrop pendant wrapped in white gold with a matching ring that ended at her knuckle.

Her earrings were also tear-drop turquoise that gleamed under the lights. Chandler's gaze quickly roved the display room. There were tall cases that showcased only one or two items. One highlighted ropes of freshwater pearls with matching pearl earrings. Another housed a round sapphire necklace. Falling like shooting stars beneath it were several bands of white gold with diamonds at their tips.

The pieces were gorgeous. Exactly the sort of one-of-a-kind jewelry that she also made.

The woman smiled. "What brings you to Vicki Orr's Designs today?"

"Are you Vicki?"

The woman pulled off her glasses and let them hang around her neck from the chain holding them. "I sure am. What can I do for you?"

Here goes nothing. "My name is Chandler Rigby, and I'm a goldsmith from New York."

Vicki pursed her lips and tipped her head. "Hmm. I've never heard of you."

Her insides wilted, and her lips trembled. But instead of cowering, she pushed forward. "I make very industrial-style pieces. But I'm here on vacation and my muse has struck! The problem is that I don't have any of my equipment here. I was wondering"—she ignored the basketball of nerves bouncing in her stomach—"would it be possible for me to rent time in your shop and pay for all supplies I would need—gold, gemstones, that sort of thing?"

Vicki's eyes narrowed. "What did you say your name is again?"

The jeweler's suspicious gaze made her wince. "Chandler Rigby. I'm all over social media."

"And you're from New York, you say."

"Yes, but I'm staying in Sugar Cove for a while, and I don't know when I'll be returning. I was hoping that I could create from here. Like I said, I'd be happy to pay you." But the more she talked, the more scrutinous Vicki's gaze became. Chandler had to say something to save herself. She brushed her fingers lightly atop one of the glass cases so as not to leave smudges. "I love those pearls. They're so beautiful."

"Thank you," Vicki said frostily. "I'm afraid that I don't have good news for you. I'm sorry, but I don't know you. I appreciate that you're willing to pay and that you're a goldsmith yourself, but my studio isn't set up for anyone but me."

Her hopes slipped away. "I understand. Thank you for your time."

She turned to go when Vicki's voice stopped her. "Wait."

Hope swelled in her chest. She turned around and smiled tentatively. "Yes?"

"Where did you study?"

Her chest deflated. "At SCAD—the Savannah College of Art and Design. Then I moved to New York."

Vicki just nodded and Chandler took that as her invitation to leave. She hunched her shoulders and scurried from the shop, embarrassment burning on her cheeks.

Now what would she do? Return to New York? But her inspiration was here. Her soul was filling up here. She didn't want to leave Sugar Cove with its beauty to return to the sharp lines and even sharper people in the city.

She liked the comfort and the slow pace of the beachside community. Did she dare even admit to herself that she could find herself living there for a while?

She looked for a tissue, and her fingers scraped over a small bundle. Oh, wow. Chandler did have one necklace with her. A quick glance at her watch told her that Vicki Orr Designs would be closing in ten minutes.

There was one shot left.

She whipped around and practically raced back across the street, holding up her hand in apology at a car that had to slow for her.

She yanked open the door and found Vicki standing exactly as she left her, behind the counter. But now the woman's eyes were wide with worry.

Chandler chose to ignore that as she gently settled the bundle on the glass-topped case and spoke while she unfolded it.

"Three weeks ago, a gallery designer, a friend of mine, told me that my art was gone. That I was all washed up. I knew it was true. I'd lost my muse, and it wasn't coming back. My mom bought a lighthouse in Sugar Cove, and I came here to help her get a restaurant up and going. But the whole time I've been empty. I can't live up to my boyfriend's family's expectations as a partner for him, and two days ago I was on a boat and saw all these amazing seashells and suddenly, just like that, my muse was back."

She stared at the delicate gold-wire wrapped gemstones and sighed.

"This is what I used to create, but this"—she pulled her sketchpad from her purse and flipped the page to a design made of delicate sapphires jointed together in a delicate chain of butterflies—"is what I *need* to create. I don't have anything else. Well, other than my family. But this is my life, and for weeks I felt like I had lost it. I only want it back."

She exhaled a gusty sigh and waited, her nerves firing against her skin on all cylinders.

Vicki picked up the necklace and nodded. Then she glanced at the sketchpad and frowned. Chandler's insides squeezed. That was it. It was over.

She'd given this her best and only shot.

Vicki studied the sketch for a moment longer, and Chandler put it back into her purse, defeated. She waited for the goldsmith to place the necklace back on the counter, and when she did, Chandler wrapped it up.

"Thank you for your time," she said, turning to leave.

"Wait." Vicki cleared her throat. "When do you want to start?"

CHAPTER 29

Ginny

"I'm so glad you called. I've been thinking about you."

Ginny sat across from Molly at Provisions restaurant in downtown Port St. Joe.

Molly smiled at her while running a finger over her glass of white wine. "How's the café? I have to tell you, I thought it was wonderful, absolutely some of the best food I've eaten in ages. And so much comfort!" She clasped a hand to her breast. "Really just reminded me of home cooking. You know, these fancy places are great"—she gestured to the tasteful decorations in Provisions—"but sometimes I just want macaroni and cheese. Can't you tell by my waistline?"

Ginny swatted at her playfully. "Molly, you're gorgeous. Always have been."

"Tell my ex-husband that." Her gaze roved the front door as it opened. "Oh, there's my daughter, Paige, and her boyfriend. Let me call them over."

She waved and a beautiful young woman with long brown hair holding the hand of young man—both of whom looked to be in their twenties—came over.

Paige had a lovely round face and warm almond-colored eyes. "I've heard so much about you," she gushed. "Mama talks about you all the time and about what fun y'all had as sorority sisters."

"Yeah, I have to hear about it too," said Blake, the young man holding her arm.

Ginny's eyes narrowed at Blake's tone. He was good-looking with a honey-colored complexion and hazel eyes, but she couldn't quite get over the way he'd spoken to Paige, as if hearing about the past was a burden.

"We were just about to eat," Paige said. "They have the best goat cheese marinara."

"That's what I'm getting," Ginny said. "I'm glad to know it's good."

"You can't go wrong with anything on the menu," she assured her.

"And unless I stop you, you'll eat it all," Blake said, his tone semi-serious.

Paige's cheeks tinged pink, and her gaze darted to the floor. "We won't keep y'all. Nice to meet you."

"Same here."

Once they were out of earshot, Molly leaned over. "Paige is sensitive about her weight."

"She's a beautiful young woman," she said, honestly meaning it. "Have she and Blake been dating long?"

Her old friend frowned. "A bit too long, if you ask me." She shifted in her seat, and Ginny knew the cutting voice that she'd thought she'd imagined coming from Blake hadn't been her imagination at all. "Sometimes I think he only dates her to feel better about himself. He's in real estate and things have been tough lately, from what Paige tells me."

She patted Molly's hand. "It'll work itself out."

"I know." Molly inhaled a deep shot of air and ran her fingers through her curly platinum locks. "These things always do. It's just hard being her mother and watching, not knowing exactly when to intervene."

"You'll know when the time's right."

"I guess so. Oh, look. Our food's here."

Ginny was watching her pocketbook, so she'd only ordered the goat cheese marinara fondue appetizer and it didn't disappoint. Yummy marinara sprinkled with creamy goat cheese and eaten on freshly made garlic bread was a real treat.

"Molly, is that you?"

An older gentleman, early sixties, with his hair slicked back, approached the table. He wore a dark suit and had an angular face, the sort of face, she thought with amusement, that should have belonged to a villain in a movie.

There was no malice in his eyes, but his features were so sharp that it took her a moment to get the mental image of him as a villain out of her mind.

"Reynold Thompkins." Molly extended her hand. Reynold took it and squeezed before releasing his hold. "I haven't seen you in forever." She gestured to Ginny. "This is my friend, Ginny Rigby."

Reynold's eyebrows curled with interest. "Rigby? You wouldn't happen to be the woman who runs the Lighthouse Café, would you?"

She beamed. "Proud owner, that's me."

"Wonderful," he purred. "I've been meaning to stop by."

"We'd love to have you."

"From what I understand, your menu is rather...rustic."

The way he said the word *rustic* sent a shiver shimmying down her spine. A knot welled in her throat, but she forced herself to smile. "Yes, it's comfort food. I'm working my way through the Magnolia Sisters Cookbook."

His eyebrows shot to stiff peaks. "Magnolia Sisters? I'm familiar with it. Used to be, there wasn't a Southern kitchen that didn't have that cookbook on the counter."

She beamed with delight. "I never got the chance to cook much of it...before. But now I'm exploring it and using it for my menu. You know it?"

"My dear"—he leaned forward and his presence ate up her entire line of sight—"my mother was one of the original recipe creators for that book."

Excitement bubbled up in her. "You don't say! Which recipe was hers?"

"Ethel's chicken and dumplings."

She gasped with delight. "Wonderful! That's on my list to make next week. I try to keep a balance of seafood and comfort food, but I will be making that on Wednesday. You should stop by. We'd love to have you."

He pressed a hand to his heart. "I would love to." He turned to Molly. "Wonderful seeing you."

They said goodbye and Ginny could not believe her luck. "I can't believe his mother was one of the contributors to that cookbook. What are the odds?"

But Molly didn't look pleased at all. In fact, she kept her gaze firmly on her bowl of pasta.

"What is it?"

"Well, I don't know how to tell you this." Molly took a long sip of tea as if to secure her courage. "But there's something you should know about him."

"Okay," she said slowly. "What is it?"

"He's a food critic."

Oh. Ginny laughed lightly. "Well, at some point the café will have to be reviewed by a professional, don't you think? The reviews on Yelp so far are great, so I'm not too worried."

Molly still wasn't looking at her. "Reynold is sort of in his own category of critics."

"What do you mean?" she asked, taking a bite of goat cheese. It took Molly a long moment to answer, and her brow began to sweat. "Molly? You're beginning to scare me."

"I'm sorry." She glanced up and smiled tightly. "I'm not trying to, but I think you should know."

"What?"

She settled her fork on her plate and dabbed her napkin to both sides of her mouth. If Ginny didn't know any better, she would think that Molly was stalling for time. But why?

She didn't have to wait long for the answer, because her friend cleared her throat. "You should know that the last three restaurants that Reynold has given poor reviews to haven't done well at all."

A nervous trill of laughter escaped her throat. "What do you mean by that? They lost a little business?"

Molly shook her head, and a storm brewed in her eyes. "It's not that they just didn't do well. They closed. Permanently."

CHAPTER 30

Reece

"We are going to have so much fun," Shelby said as she pulled her inside the bar. The place was packed, the lights were dim and the band was jamming.

Reece had to shout to be heard. "Where are your friends?"

"Upstairs playing pool. Come on, I can't wait for you to meet them and *him*," Shelby said, tugging her strawberry-blonde locks over one shoulder. "How do I look?"

She looked beautiful with her pouty lips and smoky eyes. She looked so pretty that Reece suddenly felt like a wallflower next to her. She needed to check her own makeup to ensure everything was in place. Shelby had applied it, but Reece had a habit of wiping her fingers over her eyes, smudging any shadow.

"I'm going to hit the bathroom. I'll meet you upstairs," she told her friend.

Shelby squeezed her hand. "Okay, but don't be gone too long or I'll come looking for you, thinking some man grabbed you."

Reece chuckled. As if that would happen.

She slinked to the bathroom and found herself in line with ten other women all applying lipstick and fixing their hair. She stared at herself. She'd picked a simple T-shirt and cut off shorts. The nights were still warm enough to get away with shorts even though October was edging in.

Her lips looked pale, and she applied a coat of pink lipstick. Her eyeliner *was* running, and from the looks of the heavily made-up women, if Reece wanted to compete, she needed a little help.

She dug out her emergency makeup bag and darkened her eyes, smudging them on the corners like Shelby. She pulled her brown hair over one shoulder and smiled. Satisfied with how she looked, Reece exited the bathroom. A woman was coming out right behind her, and she held the door as she stepped out, not looking to see where she was going.

Splat! She heard the drink splash across her shirt before she felt it.

Reece sucked air and stared down. The bottom of her shirt and top of her shorts were soaked through.

"I'm so sorry," a man said, his voice thick with apology. "Hey, I know you."

She glanced up into bright blue eyes that searched her, peered into her. There was more—sandy hair that was swept to one side, a strong jaw, straight nose, perfect teeth, and broad shoulders.

Her heart flailed in her rib cage in a wild attempt to leap from her chest.

It was *him*. The runner she said hello to nearly every morning. Oh my God. He was here. She wanted to dart under a table. Her clothes were soaked with beer. There was probably beer in her hair, too. She smelled like hops and yeast instead of vanilla and sugar.

He settled the empty beer glass down and grabbed her by the arm. "Come on. Let's get you cleaned up."

"No, no," she started to protest but then realized how stupid that sounded. What was she going to do? Walk around wet and miserable?

He took her hand without a word, and instantly a spark of fire ignited to her shoulder. Was that real or just her imagination?

She stayed close to him as they wove through the crowd. He looked back several times as if to make sure she was still with him and she was. She was touching him! They were holding hands.

Sort of.

He pulled her to the side of the bar and said something to the bartender, who handed him a key. "Thanks," he told the man.

Then he gave Reece a smile that made flames lick up her cheeks and her gaze dart to the floor.

"This way," he murmured close to her ear.

And then he lightly tugged her down a back hall and unlocked a door. He smiled again. Reece knew that somewhere, angels were singing. "Don't be worried; contrary to popular belief, there aren't monsters hidden here."

She giggled behind her hand and then realized that it smelled disgusting, so she dropped it.

"Voila!"

He stepped aside so she could see. Behind the door was a very nice private bathroom. He strode in and hit the hand dryer. The sound of blasting air filled the room.

"You can use this to dry off, and there are towels there." He pointed to a stack. "I'll be outside."

He left and the door clicked shut. She had no idea if she was supposed to be here. Would she get in trouble? But warm air sounded like a miracle for how soaking wet she was.

She stepped into the jetty of air and let it blow until her clothes were dry enough, hitting the button a couple of times when the blower screamed to a stop.

After wetting a towel and dabbing it to her face, she reapplied her makeup and put her hair under the air to give it some volume.

When the dryer went off, she slowly opened the door and peeked out. He stood in the hallway, waiting for her. His back was pressed to the wall, and his arms were folded. He looked up at her from under his lashes, and Reece fell into the warmth of his eyes.

"Hi," she said. "Thank you."

"I'm sorry about that."

"You made up for it."

He smiled and silent tension billowed up around them. "I'm Ted."

"Reece."

He dropped his head back onto his shoulders and studied the ceiling. "You cook and your name even comes from food."

She laughed. "You don't know if what I cook is any good, though."

"I've been meaning to find out."

She wasn't going to let him get off that easily. "You hadn't even told me your name until now."

Ted ran a hand over his neck. "I'm sorry about that. I meant to, but then a lot of time passed—"

"And it became uncomfortable and embarrassing to ask for it," she finished.

His brow arched. "How'd you know?"

"I felt the same thing," she confessed.

He laughed. "Busted."

He looked at her then, his face wide open, and her heart tightened. She felt an immediate bond with Ted. How was that even possible?

"Do you have a last name, Reece?"

She was still staring at him and realized that she was downright daydreaming about his face. Luckily she heard the question and managed to snap out of her reverie in time to reply, "Rigby."

"Talmadge," he told her.

"Theodore Talmadge?"

"It's terrible, isn't it?" he said in a Southern drawl that sounded sweeter than birdsong to her ears. "That's what I get being born into a Southern family. Same as you."

She chuckled. "Should we just stand in this hallway all night?"

"I could," he said in a way that made little prickles of delight dance down her flesh.

As much as Reece wanted to hang out and gawk in a hallway all night long, she did have friends waiting for her. "I'm here with people."

His eyes flared. "Me too. Maybe we should tell both our parties that we've formed another one."

It was as if he was reading her mind! "No, I can't do that."

Ted placed a hand to his chest. "Then my one goal tonight is to finally learn everything about you."

"You could do that in the mornings, on your run."

Worry filled his eyes but vanished almost as quickly as it had flared. "My time's limited in the mornings."

"Then I guess this hallway will have to do," she said taking a step forward.

"I'd better move fast, then." *Was that a glint of amusement in his eyes?* "What brought you to Sugar Cove?"

"How do you know I haven't lived here all my life?" Was she flirting? Reece never flirted. She was all book smarts and seriousness.

He laughed. "Because I know everyone, having grown up here, and you, Reece Rigby, are the mystery woman in the lighthouse."

She dropped her head back and laughed. It was a good guttural sound that made all the tension in her body float away. "You make me sound like a ghost."

"You are very much *not* a ghost."

"Okay, then." She realized the end of the hall was coming up, so she slowed her step. Ted halted as well, matching her pace. "My mom bought the lighthouse after my dad died a few months ago."

"And you're her baker?"

"Something like that." Her stomach twisted as a voice in her head shouted, *You're in medical school. Tell him that!* "I'm here helping her for as long as she needs me. We're originally from Atlanta."

"I thought I recognized your accent."

"You spend a lot of time in Georgia?"

"Business takes me there."

She quirked a brow. "What kind of business?"

"Just managing and buying things."

They'd reached the end of the corridor, and Ted rested his hand on the brick wall. The sound of the band was growing loud, and Reece knew that in a few steps she'd be swallowed by the noise and her conversation with Ted, lost.

She glanced over at him and caught him staring at her. Her gaze quickly darted away, but not before she had a chance to drink in his sharp jaw, the velvety eyes.

Reece had wished to know his name and now she did. She wished for him to take her number, but she wasn't going to linger or look desperate.

But a thought did occur to her. "What was up with that bathroom?"

He winked. "It's private. Only staff have access to it."

"You work here?"

He rubbed the back of his neck shyly. "Something like that."

"Do you bartend?"

"A little of this and that." He folded his arms, sliding his hands to the side of his chest. "I was foolish not to ask your name before, and I'd be even more stupid not to ask you out now."

Her heart fluttered into her neck. "Oh, is that so?" Was the most brilliant thing she could come up with. Reece nearly smacked herself on the head. But she did manage a, "Are you asking me out?"

"Will you say yes?"

She fought the smile that threatened to explode across her face. "Yes, I will."

Ted grinned and pulled out his phone. He asked for her number, and she gave it to him. Her phone pinged. When she glanced down, Ted had sent a smiley face.

"Now you have mine."

"Got it," she told him, sliding the phone into her pocket. "I need to get back to my friends."

He gestured toward the hall opening. "After you."

She slipped through the crowd and up the stairs. Ted followed right behind. Reece's heart was full of hope and the first fluttering of something wonderful—*maybe*. He followed her to the second floor and asked if she'd like something to drink.

She told him a Coke, and he slipped off to the bar. Reece glanced around and spotted Shelby rushing over to her. She opened her mouth to tell her friend that she'd just met the hot runner she saw every morning, but Shelby spoke first.

She tucked a strand of hair behind her ear and glanced shyly at the bar. "I see you've met my secret crush."

Reece's eyes narrowed in confusion. "Who?"

Shelby grinned. "Ted. You've met Ted. He's the guy I'm crazy for."

CHAPTER 31

Chandler

She took a deep breath before pulling the mold apart. Her stomach jumped in anticipation as she tugged gently until the silicone ripped. Inside sat a ring of white gold. The body of the ring was made of ripples that represented waves. She grabbed a cloth and doused it in alcohol and then ran the cloth over the gold until it gleamed.

The metal had done exactly what it was supposed to. Light danced on the surface while the inside edges were cast in shadow, making the piece look alive even though it was cold, dead metal.

She smiled. This was what she had come to Sugar Cove for. This was what she needed. The ring was one of dozens of designs that filled her sketchbook.

She exhaled with joy and slipped it on her finger. The door to the back room opened and Vicki entered, smiling.

"All done?"

"Here. Take a look."

She slipped it off and polished it once more before handing it to Vicki, who studied it with a smile of appreciation.

"Gorgeous, simply gorgeous," she mused. "When you first showed up, I could tell you had talent, and when you showed me your website, I saw real beauty, but you were right, your work had grown cold, distant. But this piece—Chandler, it's like the ocean is taking form right on your flesh. I love it. You do beautiful work."

She beamed at the compliment. Vicki's jewelry was one-of-a-kind. The curling bezels of gold around the stones and the way she placed gems to make them seem like they were cascading—like schools of fish or tentacles falling from a jellyfish—were truly inspiring.

"Thank you," she murmured. "I appreciate it."

Vicki handed back the ring, her eyes glittering with questions. "Well, it looks like in no time you'll have a beautiful collection."

Chandler smiled. It would be gorgeous—at least she hoped so.

"But what will you do after that? Surely you'll return to New York."

She shrugged. "I really don't know. I could always stay in Sugar Cove."

"You could...but what will you be leaving behind?"

"Leaving behind?" She polished the ring one more time before setting it on a swatch of velvet. "In New York?"

The older woman laughed and sat on an empty stool. "Come, Chandler. You and I both know you're much too beautiful and talented to only be leaving a studio. I can sense a broken heart when I see one."

"Oh, that. Yes, there is someone. But it's complicated."

She quirked a brow, and Chandler realized that sometimes it was easier to confess your sins to someone you didn't know rather than someone you did. There was less judgment involved.

Vicki threaded her fingers around one of her knees. "When I was your age, I was busy, so busy, so determined to make it that nothing was going to stand in my way—not even love. There was a man who loved me very much. He was successful here in town, but he'd been given the opportunity to leave for a different city to develop a new company. He asked me to go with him." She glanced to the ceiling with a thoughtful expression on her face. "Well, my life was here. I was building my art, my business. I'd only just opened my shop. I couldn't just leave, but I loved him. So I made a choice."

Chandler suspected that she knew what Vicki would say next, but she didn't interrupt her.

The jeweler took a deep breath. "I stayed. I let the love of my life walk out the door, heartbroken, of course, because I wouldn't go with him, and I stayed here and built my business." She released her hands and opened her palms. "I've built a great shop. People buy my jewelry from all over the world. I've been blessed."

"You certainly have been."

Vicki poked the air. "But I tell you there's one thing that I always missed and that was him. In hindsight I could've left with him. I could've built my business anywhere, but I was too afraid to lose myself." She rose and sucked in a deep breath. Her gaze roved over the ring one last time. "If I could give you one piece of unsolicited advice, it would be this: don't turn your back on love. It's more important than you think. You don't want to wake up twenty years from now and realize that you made the biggest mistake of your life."

She turned to leave the room, but Chandler stopped her. "What if... what if I need to prove something to myself first?"

Vicki shrugged. "Just make sure that whatever it is you need to prove, that you're doing it for the right reasons."

With that, she left, leaving Chandler to wonder something. Was she trying to prove to Hudson that she was good enough for him, or was she trying to prove to herself that she was good enough?

And did both of those questions lead to the same answer?

CHAPTER 32

Ginny

By the time Wednesday arrived her entire body was tight with worry.

"Everything okay, Mama?" Reece asked, sliding past her holding two plates stacked with chicken swimming in savory sauce topped with homemade dumplings.

Ginny had rolled the dough for the dumplings just that morning, working her worry into the flour. She flattened it into a disk and then cut out strips before dropping those into the bubbling broth simmering with tender chicken.

She glanced up from the empty plate she was staring at and smiled. "Yes, everything's fine."

"Then why're you staring at that plate?" Chandler asked, sweeping past her carrying two tall, iced teas.

"I'm not." She smiled tightly. "I'm serving guests."

But her nerves and her stomach had been a mess ever since her night out with Molly when they'd run into Reynold. Just thinking that one man could make or break her restaurant made her insides freeze. The pressure was nothing like she'd ever felt before.

"Head's up," Reece said, coming back into the kitchen. "Aiden's here."

"Think he wants to take you treasure hunting?" Chandler joked.

Ginny felt her cheeks burn as Reece said, "I would go treasure hunting again. That was fun and not what I expected. Who thought you just swung a magnet into the ocean and scrape it along the bottom?"

Her youngest had been grumpy ever since Friday, but the mention of Aiden and treasure hunting had seemed to lift her spirits. Ginny was glad.

"I have an idea," she said. "Why don't we have dinner tonight? Just us girls."

"Sure," Reece said.

Chandler nodded. "I'd love to."

She smiled and brushed a loose strand of hair from her face. She quickly ladled chicken and dumplings onto the plate she held and headed into the dining room. She dropped it off and smoothed her hands down her apron as she made her way to Aiden's table.

"Hey, stranger," she joked.

Aiden glanced up and smiled. The corners of his eyes fanned in a way that made her heart stutter. She was beginning to feel like she was on the upward turn in the stages of grief. She'd gone through the anger and bargaining and had whittled her way through the loneliness by cooking and serving food at her café.

Now things were looking up.

"How've you been?" he asked.

She smiled. "Well, great except today could be the end of my business." Ginny tried to make it sound like a joke, but she knew that she'd fallen flat. She exhaled a gusty sigh. "A food critic is coming today."

"Reynold decided to try out your place?"

Her stomach somersaulted. "You know him?"

He chuckled and she wasn't sure if she should be annoyed and swat him with a towel or be relieved. "Yes, Reynold. Everybody knows him. Trust me, Ginny"—her name on his lips made a shiver shimmy to her toes—"your food is great. You've got nothing to worry about."

She wished that she could share his confidence. The most she could muster was a, "Thanks."

"I would like some dumplings," he told her. "But I also came to see if you'd like to have dinner."

"Oh, I don't—"

"As a friend," he explained. "Just friends. No strings attached."

Her face flushed under his gaze. She could say no, and Farrah would kill her for it. Ginny wasn't ready for anything, she knew that. But a companion, someone other than her daughters to talk to, might not be such a bad thing.

"Okay," she said, silently praying her beating heart couldn't be heard above the murmur of chatting customers in the café. "That sounds nice."

They set up a date, and just as she was gliding away from his table, trying not to feel like she was on cloud nine, the front door opened and with it came a hot breeze and a tall shadow.

The dining room instantly quieted as Reynold stepped into the café. The heels of his shoes clacked against the tile floor, seeming to echo against the walls.

Ginny felt the hot wind wrap around her neck and squeeze as his eyes landed on her.

"Miss Ginny," he said coolly. "What a lovely café you have here."

"Thank you. Let me show you to your seat."

He was late for the lunch service, but there was an empty table that had just cleared. She brought him a tall glass of unsweet tea and a plate of chicken and dumplings for Aiden.

She deposited the plate with Aiden and wished for a moment that she could enjoy the fact that he had asked her out (even if it was without strings). But the dark shadow of Reynold's presence dimmed her light.

"He's here," she whispered when she entered the kitchen.

Reece's eyes widened. "The critic?"

"Yep. It's him. He's at table five."

Chandler sneaked a glance out the swinging door. "Five? That's him? Oh, wow. We're in trouble."

Her heart clenched.

Reece pushed past her sister with a scoff. "Don't be ridiculous. How bad could it b— Oh my. Yep, we're in trouble. Mama, I hope those chicken and dumplings are the best that have ever walked the earth."

Chandler grimaced. "He does look very, um, stern."

Her heart deflated to flattened. "I wasn't just making it up, was I? About how cranky he looks."

"Nope, you were right on the money," her youngest told her. "He looks about as grumpy as grumpy can get."

"Good thing the chicken and dumplings is getting rave reviews." Chandler took two empty plates from a shelf and scooped the savory dish onto it. She lifted one plate to her nose and inhaled. "I can't wait to try it."

That made the ache in Ginny's heart die down a bit. But it all came screeching back when Reece handed her a plate piled high with food.

"Good luck, Mama. You can do this."

Reece's words reverberated inside her. She *could* do it. She'd already done so much—started a new business and said yes to a date with a handsome treasure hunter.

If she'd been twenty years younger, Ginny would've swooned at the thought.

Chandler placed both hands on her shoulders. "You've got this."

"I've got this," she repeated.

Before she could think a single negative thought, her feet were pointed toward the kitchen door and she was walking out into the dining room, beelining straight for Reynold's table.

"Here you are," she said, delivering a plate of steaming chicken swimming in a thick broth. Strips of white dumplings were crisscrossed over the poultry, and he took a long moment to sniff and inspect the plate.

"Thank you," was all he said.

"Enjoy."

"Mm hm," he replied, which made her heart go cold. Was that all he had to say? Just, "Mm hm?" What sort of reply was that?

Ginny squared up her shoulders and went back to work. By the time the early lunch service was finished and plates were collected and patrons had paid, she had nearly forgotten about Reynold.

Aiden paid and left. Their gazes lingered on one another as they said goodbye, a silent promise of what would come next for them.

Ginny had finished depositing dishes into the kitchen and went over to ask the critic how things had gone, but the he had left.

His chair was empty, and he'd dropped money on the table to cover his bill. But that was all—there was no note, no nothing.

She didn't know if that was good or bad.

"Well?" Reece asked, coming up beside her as she wiped her hands on a towel. "Did he say anything?"

She lifted her hands in confusion. "No, I didn't talk to him. Did he finish his meal?"

Chandler entered from the kitchen. When all eyes landed on her, she grimaced. "I cleared his plate, and I don't remember how much he'd eaten. Sorry. I guess I've just got a lot on my mind."

"It's okay," Ginny assured her, though her stomach twisted into several knots. "I'm sure he enjoyed it."

"How could he not?" Reece smiled tightly. "You make the best food ever."

"Then why do you look constipated?" Chandler asked her sister.

"I look that way because I've got other things on my mind."

"What things?" Ginny asked as she pushed up her sleeves and prepared to wash dishes before the second service.

Her youngest just shrugged. "Nothing important."

As Reece walked off with a towel in hand to wipe down the tables, Ginny had the feeling that what was bothering her was quite important.

It was most important indeed.

CHAPTER 33

Reece

Reece had not been lying. She did have something on her mind. Or a *someone*, to be more accurate.

Ted had called her the day before, and she had been completely unsure what to do. Tell him they couldn't date? Be honest with him about how Shelby felt about him? Tell Ted she had a terrible illness and would die? Maybe he'd never come back to the café to see if she had actually passed away.

They were all terrible ideas.

"What do you think of this one? That would look so good on you. The burgundy goes great with your coloring."

Shelby lifted a silk blouse. Reece was yanked from her reverie and back into the now, where she was currently hanging out with Shelby in the bedroom of her grandmother's house.

Shelby was trying to find the perfect outfit for Friday night while Reece was trying to figure out the perfect way to tell her the truth about Ted.

"Here." She thrust the blouse in Reece's empty hands. "Try it on. I think it'll be perfect with jeans."

Her chest ached from the pressure of keeping a secret. That was how secrets were—they were like bricks being stacked inside of a person's body, slowly smothering them.

"I don't know if I can make it," she said. "Listen, Shelby—"

"Ted will be there," she said, her eyes dreamy. "What did you think of him? You never said."

"He seemed...nice."

Her friend dropped onto the bed and kicked off her sandals. "He's great. A wonderful man. You know he's got a daughter."

"He does?" her mouth dropped. "A daughter?"

"Yeah. She's his whole life. I've known Ted forever, but I don't think he'll ever notice me." A line of worry wrinkled Shelby's brow. "Do you?"

Reece felt like she'd been sucker punched. Her mind was still whirling from the fact that Ted had a daughter. Was that why he had to get back to his house every morning? Why he couldn't stay and chat?

The past couple of days Reece had managed to hide inside the café when it was time for Ted to run past. He probably thought she was playing hard to get when in reality she was trying to completely avoid him.

Shelby was staring at her, waiting for an answer to her question. "He'll notice you." She marched over to the closet. "Come on. We're going to find killer clothes for you." While they were scanning her wardrobe, she had a thought. "If Ted has a kid, what's he doing hanging out at a bar at night? Seems like a weird thing to do."

"It would be if it wasn't his bar."

Reece couldn't catch her breath. "He owns the bar we went to?"

It made so much sense now. Why he knew about the secret bathroom and how the bartender so easily handed him the key.

"Yeah, he owns it." The redhead raked hangered shirt after shirt over the steel bar in her closet. "Oh, I've forgotten about this." She unhooked an emerald-colored silk blouse and smoothed it over her chest. "What do you think?"

The color was perfect against her creamy skin, and it made her red hair really pop. Also, her blue eyes took on the slightest hint of green from the blouse. All in all, it would make Shelby into a knockout. Add a little smudgy eyeshadow and Ted wouldn't be able to help *but* to notice her.

"It's perfect," Reece confirmed. "I'll come over Friday night and help you get ready."

Her smile faded. "You're not coming out?"

"No, I don't think so. I've got some things to help my mother with.

But y'all go and have a great time. I can't wait to hear what Ted says when he lays his eyes on you."

Shelby squealed with delight. "You really think this outfit will nab him?"

"I do, indeed."

An hour later she was heading back to her house, her heart heavy from sadness but also from feeling fulfilled in helping Shelby. Shelby was a great friend. The last thing that Reece would do was betray her trust.

Which was why there was something that she had to do no matter how much it hurt.

She pulled her phone from her purse and dialed Ted's number. He picked up on the first ring.

"Hello?"

Just the sound of his voice made Reece want to blurt out, *You have a kid? You own a bar? You're a hot single dad who helped me get cleaned up after spilling beer on me? Why couldn't I have met you before Shelby?*

But she didn't say any of those things. Instead she replied, "Hey."

"Waited two days to call back. I would've done the same," he joked.

As much as she wanted to flirt, this wasn't the time. "I'm sorry. I've had some things going on."

Concern filled his voice, and it made her heart tighten to bursting. "Everything okay?"

"Yeah, it's all good, but listen"—she took a deep breath and prepared herself to drop the bad news—"there's a reason why I'm calling."

Reece had spent a great deal of her life not having a voice, letting her father speak through her. And though telling Ted they couldn't go out wasn't what she wanted to do, she found courage in the fact that she was doing it for Shelby.

"Uh-oh," Ted said, his voice light like he was trying to find amusement in the dread that she knew must've inflected her own speech, "sounds like I'm about to be rejected."

The fact that he sounded so light about it made it all that much worse. Because she wasn't a rocket scientist, but she understood having to mask your feelings. She'd been doing it her entire academic career.

"I'm afraid that I'll have to pass on a date. It's not that I don't want to." *I really, really want to.* "It's just that it's not a good time for me."

"Okay."

He didn't say anything else, and that made her think that she should continue word vomiting, and so she did. "I had this old boyfriend, and we had a terrible breakup. Not that he was mean or anything, but I haven't been able to get over it. Then he called me out of the blue and he wants to get back together." She gulped down a knot in her throat. "So do I."

Her lie sounded horrific. Her ex-boyfriend practically dumped her, and when he opened his arms, she leaped right back into them? He wasn't even a real person and already Reece didn't like him.

"I understand," Ted said quietly, and the smallness of his voice shattered her heart, because she knew that his was breaking same as hers.

It was almost worse to lose something that you'd never had, she suspected, than it was to lose something familiar. Because the unknowing, the spark of possibility, that hope dying was like drowning.

And that was how Reece felt—as if she were drowning. But there was no life raft that would float within arm's reach. She would have to claw her way back to shore—alone.

"I'm sorry."

"'t's okay, Reece. Goodbye."

And with that, Ted hung up.

CHAPTER 34

Ginny

S
he scooped up a spoonful of cold artichoke chicken salad and dropped it onto Chandler's plate. The dish was simple, made of Rice-a-Roni for heartiness, mayonnaise for added creaminess, and Italian dressing to give it zing. The artichokes and chicken were both mild flavors, not encroaching on the depth that the dressings added to the dish.

It was also perfect with white wine. "Girls, I'm so glad that we're doing this."

They sat outside behind the lighthouse, where Ginny had set up a wrought-iron table and cushioned chairs that Molly had sold to her for a steal.

The sun was setting and the breeze off the ocean brought with it saltiness that coated her lips when she licked them.

Reece picked at her food. Her fork stabbed a rice grain, and she slowly brought it to her lips.

"Something wrong, honey?"

"No. Yes." Her gaze snapped up and met her mother's. "Did you find out anything from the critic?"

She was trying not to think about it, but every waking hour had pretty much been spent begging God for a decent review.

"It hasn't come out yet," she admitted.

"You don't have anything to worry about, Mama," Chandler told her.

Her insides shrank just thinking of Reynold's sour face. "I hope he liked it. Because if he didn't..."

Reece sat up then and clasped a hand over her mother's. Warmth spread from her daughter's flesh into hers, and she immediately felt comforted.

"Mama, he loved it. You have a great café. Sugar Cove residents love it. Even if he didn't like his chicken and dumplings, that's not going to kill your business. No way. I'm staying and fighting."

She laughed at her daughter's gumption. "You can't. You've got school."

"Right."

Reece's gaze dropped to her food, and sadness settled over her. Ginny knew something was wrong, and like any good mother, she knew the one way to get her daughter to open up.

"I have something to confess," she said, taking a sip of wine. She would need the courage.

"What's that?" Chandler asked.

"Yeah." Reece's brow pinched in confusion. "What do you have to confess?"

"Well"—she took a deep breath, holding it as long as she could because she couldn't hold her breath and speak at the same time—"Aiden asked me out. It's not quite a date. But I said yes."

Chandler finished nibbling on a bite of food and smiled. "I think that's great."

Her heart leaped from her chest. "You do?"

"Yes. Mama, you can't be alone forever, and we know how Dad was."

"What do you mean?" Had they found out about the second family?

"He never let you have any fun." She sipped her wine and gently placed the glass on the table. "He played golf while you made sure the house ran smoothly. You had to shop second-hand while he wore hand-made suits. You deserve happiness."

She couldn't believe what she was hearing. "You do think so?"

"Yes, of course. It's not like you're ready to fall in love with anybody, but you do deserve to have a little fun. You can't hole yourself up in the café day in and out."

No, she couldn't. Chandler was right about that. Ginny deserved to meet someone. "I'm not looking for anything romantic," she told her daughters sharply, so that they would know exactly where she stood on the topic of love. "But Aiden seems nice."

"And he is a treasure hunter," her youngest told her, a sly smile quirking her lips.

Now *she* was the hard one, the steel wall who would be more difficult to pierce, to convince that seeing him didn't mean the end of the world.

"Chandler's right," Reece added. "You deserve to have some fun."

"Oh, girls, you don't know how relieved I am."

Chandler smiled kindly. "The three of us have been spending a lot of time together, but we haven't been completely honest with one another."

She was worried now. What was this about? The three women should've been coming together during this time, but there were black clouds hanging over all of them.

"What's going on?" she asked.

"I broke up with Hudson," her eldest admitted, releasing a shaky breath. "I couldn't keep him, not the way I was feeling. It wasn't fair to him."

"You broke up?" Reece shot out. "You broke up with Mr. Perfect because, why again?"

Chandler pinched the bridge of her nose and shut her eyes. "Because I couldn't live up to his standards."

"Are you sure they were his standards or were they yours?" her youngest prodded.

"You don't know his family like I do. They are his standards. He wouldn't have wanted me, not once he saw how my art was failing me. But now..."

"But now what, honey?"

Her shoulders started to shake. Ginny and Reece exchanged worried looks. Was she crying?

Then Chandler released a loud burst of laughter. She lifted her hands and dropped them to her sides in defeat. "But now I've got my muse back!"

"That's great," she gushed, feeling a bubble of joy fill her chest. "But it doesn't help with Hudson."

"I know." She sighed. "He's been writing me letters." She thrust a hand in her pocket and pulled out several, dumping them on the table. "It's all about undying love."

"Wow, and from a lawyer," Reece joked.

"Even lawyers have hearts."

Ginny wasn't so sure of that, but she was certain she knew how Hudson felt about her daughter. You couldn't fake the way that he looked into her eyes and opened doors for her, pressed his hand to the small of her back, protectively steering her through a crowd. Hudson adored her, but if Chandler wanted him back, she would have to eat some crow.

"What are you going to do?" she asked.

She raked her fingers through her fine blonde locks. She dropped her lithe arm to her side and exhaled a gusty breath. "I don't know. I don't think that I deserve him. I practically told him that he needed more than a washed-up jewelry designer. He needed a true match."

Ginny considered that and wondered how she could help Chandler feel surer of herself. "Honey, you are a match for any man. Losing your art doesn't mean that you deserve any less. You are worthy of a thousand Hudsons' love, and you know what? I think he knows that. That's why he's been writing to you. He just wanted you to see it."

"But I feel so awful." She rubbed the backs of her hands to her eyes. "It feels so flaky to now say, I got my muse back! I'm worthy of your love. I'll return to New York."

"Is that what you want? To go?"

She nibbled her bottom lip a moment. "No. I don't think so. This place, this ocean, this beach, this lighthouse is where I found my muse. I need to stay here."

"And what if you lose your muse again?" Reece chirped.

Chandler's gaze slashed to her sister. "I don't think I will. I needed to breathe. I needed to get away from the smog and dirt, the grime and darkness of the city. I needed beauty and the earth to replenish me."

So had she, Ginny realized. She needed a simple life running a small business in a beach town to fill her back up and make her realize that there had been more to life than Jack. Not that she regretted marrying him. She didn't. They'd made two beautiful daughters. She didn't regret one moment, and even the anger of his betrayal was slowly subsiding. The sting of it wasn't as sharp anymore. She wasn't completely over it, but distance and time did heal wounds—hers, at least.

"What are you going to do?" Reece asked Chandler. "About Hudson, I mean?"

She lifted her shoulders and let them fall with a huff. "That's just it. I don't know. I don't want to return to New York, and that's where his life is. There's no way to meet in the middle on this."

Her face crumpled in frustration, and Ginny's heart ached for her daughter. It was a terrible thing to be lost. To know that you loved someone but that you couldn't give them what they needed. That was what had broken them up. She couldn't live up to the expectations that society would put on her. But now that she had pulled herself from the dregs and was on solid ground, she still didn't see a way for them to be together.

"If the love is meant to be, it'll find a way," Ginny said.

"Unless your best friend is in love with the one you love," Reece blurted out.

"What's this?" Ginny said.

It was Reece's turn to sigh. Except in typical Reece fashion, she didn't simply sigh, she lifted her chin to the heavens and looked at the sky as if asking God why he had burdened her with whatever was weighing on her shoulders.

"There's this guy. His name's Ted," she explained. "I've seen him every morning for the past few weeks. He runs past here after I finish baking. We've talked but nothing serious. Well, Shelby invited me out last Friday."

"I remember. I didn't go," Chandler said.

"Yeah, because I guess you were busy finding your muse."

"You don't have to be so snide about it."

Reece ignored her. "Anyway, I ran into him at the bar, and we hit it off. He got my number. He called and asked me out."

"And the problem is?" Ginny asked, knowing the ending wasn't going to be roses.

"The problem is"—she scratched her head in frustration—"that Shelby's in love with him. Wants to date him so badly. And get this—Ted has his own business. He's got a daughter. I don't know how, but I imagine that he's a widower. His wife probably drowned in a tragically romantic accident."

Ginny chuckled. "For a medical student, you are quite creative."

As some who went into the medical and science fields weren't that creative, this was a compliment to Reece.

She shook her head. "But anyway, Shelby likes him, so I told him that I couldn't see him."

Chandler squinted at her sister. "What did you say?"

"Oh, you know, my long-lost boyfriend just won me back."

"Reece Rigby," Ginny gasped, "you lied to him?"

She lifted her arms. "What was I supposed to do? Just ignore his phone call? Never call him back? Ghost him?"

"Yes," Chandler and Ginny answered.

"I obviously couldn't tell him about Shelby. She'd kill me. Anyway, I had to do it. I couldn't *not* call him. That would've been worse because he runs by the café almost every day. Though now that I think about it, he hasn't been around all week."

"Because he asked you out and doesn't want to crowd you," Chandler said. "Cheer up. You did the right thing. You can't betray your friend."

"I know," she said. "But that doesn't help me feel any better."

Ginny opened her arms wide. "How can you not feel a tiny bit better? You're with your family. We love you—always have, always will. We're eating dinner together and watching the sunset."

"You're right," she said, slyly glancing at Chandler, who lifted her eyebrows. There was some silent communication going on there, but Ginny wasn't going to ask what it was. Whatever the conversation, it was between sisters.

"Come in for a hug and a picture," she demanded.

The girls rose from their chairs and flanked each side of their mother. They wrapped their arms around her as Ginny lifted her phone and took a selfie of the trio.

"That's one for the fridge," she said proudly.

Her heart was full of love, and Ginny was so happy she felt like in that moment, nothing could destroy their bond. Everything was perfect.

What could possibly go wrong?

Turned out, everything.

CHAPTER 35

Ginny

"Still no word on Reynold's article?" Aiden asked.

She cracked open a crab leg, revealing the flaky white flesh inside. "None. I have no idea what's going to happen. But you know what, I don't care. Come hell or high water, I'm building a new life here."

They sat at a beachside restaurant about an hour from her café. He had insisted on picking her up. He'd dressed in linen pants and a short-sleeved T-shirt. She wore a maxi dress that brushed her ankles.

They were alone and they were adults. Anything could happen.

"You have to promise me," he told her, "that if you ever plan to sell the lighthouse, you give me first dibs."

She cocked an eyebrow at him in surprise. "It means that much to you?"

"It means the world to me."

She slapped her hands on the table, sending crab meat flying into the air. "You should never have let me buy it."

He chuckled. "I had a lot of great memories there. In fact..."

"In fact, what?"

He shook his head, glancing down at his own plate that was smothered in grilled fish and a baked potato. "I used to leave notes in there, for my grandpa. He'd find them and write back to me."

How sweet. "Where did you leave them?"

"Up in the tower. There's a small nook between two of the boards. It's just wide enough to slip a note into."

Her throat constricted at the idea of sliding through the narrow hole up into the optic section of the tower, where the broken lantern sat. "Is it?"

His eyes narrowed in suspicion. "Have you ever been up to your tower?"

"Well, um..."

"Are you telling me that you are a tower virgin?"

She blushed. "Well, you see. It's just...the space is narrow and it's not my thing."

"You don't like the ladder at the top," he guessed.

She shivered just thinking about trying to slip through the square hole. "It feels very constricting."

He frowned but just nodded. "I can understand that. But if you would have me, I'll help you get up there."

His tenderness touched her. "Why's it so important to you?"

"Because...I guess it's because I'm a treasure hunter. I like challenges."

"I'm not a challenge."

"You sure about that?"

The heat of his gaze made warmth spread down her neck and across her chest. She suddenly found her crab legs the most intriguing thing at the table.

"I have a confession," she said.

"You hate seafood," he joked.

"No." She laughed. "My late husband." Why was she telling him this? Why was she about to relay her deepest, darkest secret to a man who was mostly a stranger? Because sometimes it was easier to talk to strangers than it was those you knew. "Jack was his name. At the reading of his will, I discovered that he had a second family, and they were inheriting my house and most of the estate. I was given one hour to pack up and leave." She laughed. It sounded a touch maniacal even to her. "That's why I ended up here in such a state and bought the lighthouse." She brushed her hands together as if washing herself free from her old life. "So that's it. That's what brought me here. Now you know all my deep, dark secrets."

His gaze searched her in a way that made Ginny feel as if Aiden was taking a deep look into her soul. "You know that you didn't do anything wrong, don't you?"

"What do you mean, wrong?" she asked, eyes narrowing.

He took her hands in his, and a shiver danced its way down the back of her spine. "What I mean is—what your husband did, he did for his own selfish reasons. Those reasons are no reflection of you."

A great deluge of emotions swept through her, then. Truth be told, Ginny had blamed herself. She'd walked down that path of the seven stages of grief, and she had felt all the guilt and blaming of herself for what Jack had done. But Aiden was right. None of it was her fault.

She hadn't realized how much she needed to hear that until this moment. She stared down at his hand as it cupped hers, enjoying the warmth of his flesh as it leaked onto her skin. The breeze picked up, and it blew Ginny's hair into her eyes. She freed it and realized that tears were wiping across her face.

She hadn't even known that she was crying.

She brushed the tears aside and laughed. "You didn't know how much baggage you were going to unpack when you brought me to dinner, did you?"

Amusement sparkled in his blue eyes. "I suspected. Who up and buys a lighthouse in a town that they'd never been to without even blinking? Only someone who needs change and needs it desperately." He smiled at her, and her heart ballooned with happiness. "You know, there's something that us treasure hunters are good at."

"What's that?" she asked.

"It's looking forward. In my business, there's no point in crying about the past. If you didn't secure a load of treasure on one run, you just may uncover the Holy Grail on the next. It's about the next trip, the next hunt. It's not about regretting what you didn't find."

"Or what you didn't have."

He tsked. "I'd say you had lots of great memories, and you're going to make a bunch more."

She smiled and felt her heart do that swelling thing again. "Yeah, I'm hoping to make a bunch more."

They toasted to that and watched as the sun sank into the sky. Just as the first colors of orange and pink were smearing across the horizon, he rose and took her hand.

"Come on."

She couldn't help but to giggle at being pulled up so quickly. "Where are we going?"

"To the lighthouse. If you've never experienced a sunset from the tower, you're missing out."

She could hardly argue with him. Indeed she didn't want to. She allowed him to pull her from the restaurant and guide her to his Jeep. They reached the lighthouse as the sky was illuminated in candy colors—blues and pinks, amethysts and orange.

They stood at the bottom of the tower, and Aiden said, "Want to try?"

She did.

They climbed up to the small hole, and he took the ladder rung in his hands and disappeared into the top.

His arm shot down. "Come on up. You won't believe how beautiful the view is."

She desperately wanted to put her feet on that ladder and shimmy into the hole to view Sugar Cove.

But her hands shook, and her legs quaked. "I...can't. Maybe another time."

Aiden didn't complain. Instead he slipped down, and they walked down and out onto the beach. The breeze crashed against her hair, tossing it across her face as they walked along the packed sand.

He pointed up at the lighthouse. "That up there, where the iron railing is, it's called the gallery."

"Oh? It's not a balcony?"

"No. But I like that. Lighthouses have their own terms for many things."

"Part of the history that I should learn."

"You don't have to start today."

A tendril of hair fell into her eyes, and he brushed it away. It was a kind touch, an intimate one, and it was a thing, Ginny realized, that she wasn't sure if she was ready for or not. She pulled back.

"We can go slow," he said, sensing her hesitation. "I don't plan on going anywhere."

She shook her head. "You've only just met me. The only things you know about me are that I have two daughters, a dead husband who betrayed me and a business that I pray will stay open even after the review comes out. Oh, and that I'm afraid to go to the top of the lighthouse."

"That's all I need," he said, his Southern drawl palpable. "I knew from the first moment I laid eyes on you that I wanted to get to know you. If it takes time, I've got it. Hell, I'm semi-retired and spend my days walking the beach and trying to figure out where my next treasure will be found."

Their gazes locked and she felt heat creep up her shoulders and burn the tips of her ears. Her heartbeat drummed in her throat, and she suddenly felt very deliciously vulnerable.

The tension of the moment thickened between them. It was a beautiful sunset in the background. The wind was blowing her hair (but not too much), and they were standing on the beach. This moment had all the pickings of a perfect kiss.

But she didn't want their first kiss to happen right after she'd retched up her painful past—a past that still smarted like a paper cut to the stomach.

She had an idea. "Where did you say that your grandfather and you used to leave notes?"

"Just inside, up in the tower."

"Let's see if we can find one. Do you remember who would've written one last? Would it have been you or him?"

He rubbed his cheek in thought. "Him, I think."

Her heart thrummed with excitement. What were the odds that Aiden would discover a note hidden from his grandfather after all this time? Very slim, she knew. But it was worth a shot to look.

They headed back to the tower. "Where's your secret spot?"

"At the top."

"I'll come with you most of the way."

She did, pressing herself to the brick as Aiden shimmied his way back up the ladder.

"I'll tell you where the spot is," he called down from the lantern room. "There are wooden panels all around. But there are a few that aren't tacked down as well. That's where we would put letters for one another."

"I may have to leave my own notes for you there, so that you can come up and read them."

"I wish you would," he told her.

At his words, a jolt of energy rocked Ginny's body. But she had to go slow. She was emotionally raw, not ready for anything even remotely hinting of a relationship.

After a moment he said, "I think something's here."

"You're kidding?"

"Nope. I found one." He came down the ladder and joined her on the stairs. "Thought I'd never get it."

"Where there's a will, there's a way," she said.

He opened a slip of yellowed paper and read. Her curiosity was getting the better of her. Finally she said, "Well? What does it say?"

When he looked up, a smile graced his face. "It says, 'Love you. Pop.'"

"Can I see?"

He held it out, and she read the sweet note. "What a nice message to find after all these years. But you should've told me about this sooner." She gently punched his shoulder. "I would've let you up to look for it."

"No. In my life if there's one thing I've learned, it's that things happen at the right time and for the right reason."

He stared at her, and Ginny felt heat rising on her cheeks. "Yes, I guess they do happen at the right time."

She handed him back the paper, and he folded it, sliding it into his pocket. "Would you be opposed if I left you a message?"

She laughed, thinking he was kidding. When she noted the serious expression on his face, she blanched. "You really want to?"

He nodded. "I do."

"Sure. I've probably got paper downstairs."

They found the paper and he wrote something. "I'm going to put this in the same spot. You'll find it easily enough, but you're not allowed to read it until you really need to, and when you can climb up into the top of the lighthouse and enjoy the beauty of our town."

She chuckled. "What does that mean?"

"It means whatever it means to you. Just read it when you're ready."

"Should I reply?"

He smirked in a way that made him look even more handsome. "Only if you intend on letting me back into your lighthouse."

"I think that can be arranged."

While they walked back toward the tower lantern room (another term she had learned from Aiden), Ginny thought of something. "Oh, Reece told me that it's rumored the lighthouse is haunted?"

"Right. She mentioned the ghost when we first met."

A spear of worry jabbed Ginny's heart. "*Are* there ghosts here?"

Aiden stopped and turned back to look at her. "Not that I've ever experienced, but Emma Grace did live here. Her father was the keeper well before my grandfather."

"She loved a fisherman?" Ginny asked.

"It's a real Romeo-and-Juliet type story of star-crossed lovers kept apart by families that hated one another."

A chill set into Ginny's bones and she shivered. "Is it true he wrecked, and Emma Grace was never seen again?"

"All true."

She smiled sadly. "I'll tell Reece. She wanted to know about the story."

Aiden crossed his arms. "There's not much after that. It was a long time ago, and if Emma Grace had lived, she'd be a very old woman."

"At least the lighthouse isn't haunted," she added with a nervous laugh.

"Trust me, I spent many a night here as a child. If it had been haunted, I would've seen something." He squeezed her shoulder affectionately. "You're safe here." They locked gazes and Ginny felt herself falling into him. She blinked to break the hold, and Aiden lifted the note. "Be right back. I've got a paper to deliver."

The idea of him leaving her a note for later made Ginny feel very warm and fuzzy, something that she had not experienced in ages with a man.

To keep her mind off daydreaming about Aiden, she moved over to the table where they kept the mail. Chandler had retrieved it earlier in the day, and Ginny hadn't had a chance to riffle through it until now.

Since it would take him a couple of minutes to climb the tower and return, she perused the small pile, stopping when she came to a letter addressed to her. It was from Tulane.

Why was she getting mail from her grown daughter's school? Perhaps there was something wrong with the funds that Jack had set up that were to be automatically withdrawn for Reece's tuition.

Concerned, Ginny opened the letter. That initial concern quickly became shock when she read exactly what was inside that letter.

CHAPTER 36
Reece

S helby had left to go out with her friends hours earlier. Chandler was busy doing Chandler things that didn't involve Reece, and her mother was busy on a date, so Reece found herself very much alone.

To make herself not feel quite so terribly lonely, she spent time in Port St. Joe at No Name Books & Gifts. But they had closed early, so she grabbed some food to go and went to the beach, where she ate alone while the sun set.

No, it wasn't the best way to spend a weekend night. In fact, it was far from it. But the alternative was to go out with Shelby and risk running into Ted, and she didn't want to do that. She would've preferred baking, but she needed a break from the kitchen, too. So the beach it was.

She'd just sat on a small hill of sand when her phone rang. "Aunt Farrah, it's been forever since we talked."

Farrah laughed. "If I was your aunt, I would need to be there visiting you. You know, to keep up with my family and such."

"I do have an aunt and she isn't here," Reece mused.

"That's because she's the sister of your no-good father." Farrah paused. "Sorry. I didn't mean to speak ill of the dead. It's just after everything that he did to your mother, I have very few kind words for that man. I'm sure you know what I mean."

Reece did not, in fact, know what Farrah meant, and she suspected that if she said the wrong thing, that Farrah would clam up and she wouldn't discover whatever the secret was about her dead father.

She decided to lure her "adoptive" aunt in. "Yeah, I know. I mean, all he ever wanted was for me to be a doctor. But did he ever ask me what I wanted to do? Nope. Not once. It was just assumed I would do what he said."

"Ugh, that's what I'm talking about," Farrah hissed. "The nerve of that man."

Reece thought Farrah was about to spill the beans, but then she circumvented. "Your mother says that you've been baking up a storm."

Crap. Now she had to get Farrah back on track. "Yes, I have. You know, it helps ease the ache of his death."

A sympathetic murmur whispered from Farrah's lips. "I'm so glad it does. But what about school?"

Okay, maybe *this* was her chance to lure her back in. "I came to the café to help Mama. I'm not sure exactly when I'm going back."

"That's good to hear," she gushed, sounding relieved. "I want you to finish medical school, of course. But your mama needs you. For a while I wasn't sure if she would make it. I mean, after she found out everything and bought that lighthouse in a rush, I visited because I was so worried. And who wouldn't have been a *mess*? I would've been. But that was just like Jack, controlling your mother's life even after his death. I thought that finally she'd have the chance to live in Buckhead the way she wanted, the way she had longed for, for years. But then he took all of that away."

Reece's head was swimming. Her mother had said that she'd purchased the lighthouse with real intention, but the way Farrah talked, it sounded like the purchase had happened on a whim.

"I was worried about her, too," she admitted, because that was the truth. "I mean, when I went home and found that strange woman in my house, I was like, what happened? But then Mama explained everything."

If Farrah didn't bite on that tidbit of information, Reece didn't know what else she could say to get information out of her.

The older woman sighed dramatically. "I know it was so hard for you to hear what your father had done. To think that all this time he'd had a second family and that he left them the house? How could he have done that to your mother?"

She couldn't have heard Farrah correctly. Her ears were clogged. She tugged on her earlobe to open the canal. "Um, right. Left her the house."

"And I can't imagine what it was like finding all of that out at the reading of the will, in public, for goodness' sake. *That woman* was there, too. It's a wonder your mother managed to pack so much given that she only had one hour to get out."

It seemed like a thousand points of light all converged at one spot in Reece's mind. It all made sense now—why her mother had moved so quickly, why she hadn't brought any furniture. She'd been forced out by a man who always had to assign everyone a part in life. Reece was going to be a doctor. Her mother was going to be kicked out of the life she'd always known. For him to have done that made her angry. In that moment she hated her father, despised what he had done.

But at the same time she was angry at her mother, feeling betrayed. Why had she kept such a secret from them?

As if Farrah could read her mind, she said, "Of course I hope you haven't been hard on your mama. Think of how embarrassing it was to have been treated that way. And the gossips have had a field day here. You know that I've put everyone in their place when I could."

"Sure," Reece said, her body numb. For some reason she couldn't feel her legs or arms. "I understand."

But she still couldn't understand why her mother hadn't told them, why she hadn't admitted to them the truth. It was a betrayal, and it wouldn't have surprised her in the tiniest bit if Chandler hadn't known the truth all along.

In fact, she probably did. It made sense. Chandler had figured out Reece's secret, and she'd told Reece to be kind to their mother, to let her go out on a date.

If her sister had been mourning their father properly, she never would've said that. Yep. Chandler knew the truth. She wanted their mother to date because she knew what Reece didn't.

And that was how it always was. Chandler was given first priority while she was swept into the corner. Just go and be a doctor, and since you're the youngest, Reece, no one really trusts you with our secrets. You're still too immature to be treated as an adult.

If she was being honest with herself, avoiding her professors was high on the immaturity list.

But Reece was not being honest with herself. She was fueled by anger, by the resentment that she'd felt all her life. She was second fiddle, second string, and never quite old enough to matter the way that she wanted to.

She couldn't even date the man she wanted because doing so would ruin a friendship, and Shelby was more of a sister to her than Chandler was. At least Shelby talked about her feelings and opened up. Chandler just looked at Reece like she wouldn't understand, and that was the way of it.

Maybe she wouldn't understand some things, but she at least deserved a chance.

"Reece? Reece, are you there?"

"Yes, Aunt Farrah, I'm here."

"Oh, good." A small laugh trilled from the back of her throat. "For a moment I thought that I'd lost you."

Reece narrowed her eyes as anger churned in her stomach. "You haven't lost me, Farrah. You haven't lost me at all."

CHAPTER 37

Chandler

The necklace was a masterpiece. Chandler had smithed five butterflies with wings made of sapphire and bodies of freshwater pearls. She also created a fine gold chain that the butterflies connected to. The piece was fragile and beautiful and unique all at once.

It was one of the best works of art that Chandler had ever created, and she was proud of it. She put it on and admired the way the pearls glinted under the lights. The sapphire wings also seemed to have a life of their own, radiating in the golden ambiance that filled Vicki's store.

Chandler shouldn't wear it. She really shouldn't. But just for a few hours, it couldn't hurt to put it on. Then she'd clean it up, make sure it was free from any scratches, and she'd add it to the collection that she was slowly creating.

She had found that her smithing required some adjusting in the humid Florida conditions. But once she'd figured out when was the right time of day to cast—better earlier than later, when the sun was up—then her pieces came out perfectly, and the few that hadn't quite taken, cracking and not filling in the molds correctly, were set aside and used as learning tools.

She admired the necklace one last time as her phone dinged. She sneaked a look and saw that it was Hudson. Her heart shriveled. How she wanted to talk to him. She ached to wrap her arms around him and tell him how wrong and selfish that she'd been, how stupid.

But she couldn't bring herself to do it. He deserved someone who was better than her, someone who didn't wither and die when they couldn't create art.

She didn't even read the text. She'd do so later, when she was alone in her room with a glass of wine and a book on her lap.

Chandler took one last look in the mirror and decided to wear the jewelry. After all, it was only for one night. She knew how to take care of her pieces. It shouldn't become scratched with only a few hours of wear.

She glanced at her watch and saw that it was getting late. Her mother was probably finished with her date, and Chandler wanted to know how it had gone. She liked Aiden, had a good sense about him. He seemed laid back and not at all like their father, which Chandler thought was a good thing.

Not that she hadn't loved her father. She had. Very much. But she saw how he controlled how much money her mother had to spend, how he managed her funds down to the penny. Sometimes, when she'd been younger, Chandler would slip some of her allowance money into her mother's wallet, just so she'd have a little extra.

And then he had practically forced Reece into medical school. How could Reece have said no? Reece had no choice in her future, but she didn't know that Chandler knew that.

Years ago Chandler had fallen asleep in a dark corner of her father's office, behind a screen with a potted plant in front of it. It was the one place where she could go where it was dark and warm, a place in the house to pile up blankets and take a nap. A spot where no one would find her.

She was perhaps early teens. Reece was maybe eleven when it had happened.

Chandler had just woken up when the office door opened.

"Sit down, Reece. I want to talk to you."

"Yes, Daddy?"

She heard the chair leather squeak as both of them sat. She contemplated leaving but was curious what her father could want. Was Reece in trouble? The only times Chandler was ever called into the office was when she was in trouble. So that was most likely the case.

What had Reece done?

"I want to talk about your future," their father said. "What you want to be when you grow up."

"Oh, I want to cook. I want to be a chef," Reece proudly exclaimed. "And have a restaurant and learn how to make pies and tarts."

"No," her father said coldly.

"I'm sorry?"

He sighed. "Reece, there are people in life who get to do whatever they want because the path they've chosen fits them. Your sister, she wants to be an artist of some sort and she can do that because we both know that Chandler will wind up married. But you—you don't have the same skill set as she does."

She peeked out from behind the screen. Reece sat with mouth open and eyes wide. Her hair into a ponytail, like it always was. She'd had her period, Chandler knew, but Reece hadn't stepped into her teenage years yet. She wasn't obsessed with boys and makeup. If she had been, Reece would've done something with her hair, would've at least learned how to apply mascara.

Chandler had tried to get her interested in those things, but Reece didn't want to learn. She wanted to watch TV and play sports. She wasn't interested in boys.

Their father continued. "That's why I've called you here today. You need a path in life that will set you up. If you get married, great. But if you don't, you're going to have a career that we're all proud of, that *you're* proud of. You're going to become a doctor. You've got the brains for it. You're smart and make good grades."

Reece's gaze swiveled around the room in confusion. "But I don't want to be a doctor."

Her father slammed his fist onto the desk. "Damn it, you will not embarrass this family. No daughter of mine will go off and become a chef. You will become a doctor or else I'll cut you off. At eighteen you'll be done and if you want to go to a good college, you'll be paying for it yourself. Do you understand?"

Reece winced and it broke Chandler's heart. "Okay," she whimpered to their father. "I'll become a doctor."

"This means a lot of studying," he told her.

She nodded without lifting her gaze from the floor. "I know."

"Are you up for the challenge?"

She wanted to jump out from behind the screen and yell at her father that of course Reece was up for the challenge. What other choice did she have?

Reece said yes and left the office. Her father exited a short while later, and Chandler slithered out from behind the screen and went to find your sister.

"Hey," she said and was about to tell her sister that she'd heard what had happened when Reece's eyes narrowed.

"Leave me alone," her sister spat. "Just leave me alone."

She slammed her bedroom door in her face. The sting had bitten into Chandler so badly that afterward, she shrank away from her younger sister. If Reece wanted to live alone in her misery, then so be it.

And so that was what Chandler was thinking when she walked into the lighthouse. The first words she heard came from Reece, who whirled on her and said in an accusing tone, "You knew the whole time, didn't you?"

CHAPTER 38

Ginny

S he did her best not to stew over the letter. But as soon as Aiden left, she reread the heavily weighted paper that had been slipped into an envelope with official Tulane letterhead.

Mrs. Rigby, the letter started. Ginny nearly snickered at that. No one had called her Mrs. Rigby in months, and for that she was grateful. The letter immediately poked at the open wound of her heart as soon as she began.

We have been trying to reach Reece Rigby. Our records state that you are her next of kin, and so we are writing to inform you that our faculty's many attempts to contact Ms. Rigby have gone ignored. Since she has failed to respond to our inquiries, we have no choice but to terminate her enrollment in the Tulane University School of Medicine.

It was signed by the dean, which felt to Ginny as if the letter were sealed in stone.

She had to think, to wrap her head around what she had just read. Reece wasn't enrolled? She wasn't planning to make up her lost time in summer school?

Reece had lied to her.

Anger bubbled inside her. Her youngest daughter had lied, had outright told Ginny that she would return to Tulane to finish medical school, but that had never been her intention.

The front door to the lighthouse opened just as she finished that thought. Furious at the betrayal, she stormed into the main room and met Reece as she was also walking with dire purpose toward Ginny.

"Why didn't you tell me?" Reece demanded.

What? Ginny was the one who was supposed to be demanding things. "What are you talking about?"

Reece rolled her eyes. So typical for her age. "About the woman, and the house and the will, Mama. Why didn't you tell me?"

Ginny felt as if she'd been hit in the chest with a pole. The air immediately left her lungs. Was that from the shock? Her hands became cold, and her neck heated from embarrassment and shame.

When she'd told Aiden everything, she hadn't felt this. Ginny had felt somewhat liberated that she'd been able to even talk to him about what had happened to her. But having her daughter sling accusations (as if Ginny *owed* it to Reece to rip her heart open and unburden her deepest shame) just honestly ticked her off.

She snatched the letter from the table and shoved it toward Reece. "Tell *you*? Why didn't you tell me about Tulane? About quitting medical school?"

Reece huffed a defiant scoff. "I didn't quit."

"Really? Because this letter says differently. It says that your teachers have tried to get in touch with you, and that you haven't responded to their repeated requests to remain enrolled. You have *quit*. How could you?"

"How could I?" she slammed her hand against her chest. "How could *you* not tell me that Daddy forced you out? That he had another family? That he has at least one child from a different woman. How could you keep that from me?"

The truths that she flung hit Ginny hard. Jack's actions had ripped her heart from her chest once, and her daughter talking about it made her heart rip out all over again.

"How could I keep it from you?" she repeated numbly. "How could I not?"

The door opened again, and Chandler stepped in. Tears blurred Ginny's vision, so she barely noticed the blue jeweled necklace dangling beneath her daughter's throat. Were those butterflies?

Reece whirled on her. "You knew the whole time, didn't you?"

Chandler's face wrinkled in confusion. "Knew what?"

"The family *secrets*," Reece spat. "It would be just like you to have known and not tell anyone. You always know things."

"What are you talking about?"

Reece threw up her hands. "You were always Daddy's favorite. Beautiful perfect Chandler who could never do any wrong. Who didn't have to go to medical school because she wasn't mousy and not so pretty. Who got to do whatever she wanted at all times. Even now you're doing what you want. You're running off and creating jewelry while I wake up at two a.m. to bake."

Chandler winced under Reece's attack. "Look, no one is forcing you to wake up that early." She frowned. "This isn't about me, Reece. Whatever your problems are, they're your fault." Her gaze landed firmly on Ginny. "You finally found out about Reece and school, didn't you?"

How had everyone known except her? Had they both kept this secret thinking that she would never find out the truth? "You knew about it?"

Chandler tipped her head sympathetically. "It was obvious. Reece isn't interested in going back to medical school. The only reason why she ever went in the first place was because Daddy made her go. Told her she had to."

It felt like a hand reached inside of Ginny's chest and squeezed her heart until it was about to burst. She gazed at Reece through her blurry vision. "You never wanted to go?"

Her youngest burst into tears. They were big sopping sobs that lasted several long moments before she inhaled sharply, straightened her back and knuckled the tears from under her eyes. With a staggering breath she said, "I hate medical school. I hate everything about it. I don't want to be a doctor. I've never wanted it. But I had to do what Daddy wanted, and even after he died, I felt like I had to keep doing it or else he would've been looking down on me with disappointment."

That was rich. Jack disappointed in *them*? They were the ones who should've been disappointed in their father and his philandering ways.

But before Ginny could say a word, Reece snapped at Chandler. "All I ever wanted to be was perfect, like you. But I always came up short. Is that why you hate me so much?"

"I don't hat—"

"Of course you do!"

Reece did always like to be alone in her misery. She wasn't one for company, a point Ginny had realized a long time ago when after Reece's favorite doll broke. She tried to hug her, but Reece just pushed her away. Nothing had changed. She wouldn't unburden her sadness on Ginny then and she wasn't doing it now either.

Chandler reached for her sister to console her, but Reece lifted her hand to slap her away. Her fingers curled as they arched through the air, bent like claws as they swiped at Chandler.

In hindsight, Ginny didn't think that Reece meant to wreak the havoc that she did. She had to believe that, because when Chandler realized that her sister's fingers were coming for her, she turned away.

But it wasn't fast enough. Reece's fingers grazed through Chandler's hair and snagged onto the beautiful blue butterflies (Ginny's tears had dried enough for her to correctly identify them) that wound like delicate lace around her neck.

The chain broke and the necklace crashed to the floor. The butterflies shattered apart. Sapphires and pearls skidded across the tile.

All three women stared at the wreckage.

Ginny's breath caught. Her gaze flicked to Chandler, whose eyes brimmed with horror. "I worked... It was my best piece. I was going to show it to y'all, to the world."

Regret overflowed from Reece's voice. "I'm so sorry. I didn't mean to do that. Please forgive me." She dropped to the floor and started picking up the pieces, scrabbling across the tile to reach for a pearl that had rolled under a chair. "I'm so, so sorry."

Ginny sank to the floor as well, her heart broken for herself and for her daughters. The pain that they had both endured quietly speared her. She had never wanted her daughters to be so distant. All she'd ever yearned for was a close-knit, loving family.

Now they were just as broken as the shattered necklace.

She picked up a wing, placed it in her palm and studied the brilliant sapphire.

And then she laughed.

It was a small noise, tiny at first, bubbling from her very core. It could have been mistaken for a sob, and probably was from the way both of her daughters glanced guiltily toward her.

But it wasn't.

In fact, the laughter built, becoming strong as a tidal wave as it pushed up through her throat and burst from her mouth like water spewing from a sink.

Then tears mixed with the laughter and Ginny was euphorically giddy with sadness and joy—joy to be with her daughters when the three of them were all so broken, and sad that she hadn't told them one tiny crumb of the truth as to why she'd escaped to Sugar Cove in the first place.

She lifted a wing and pearl. "We're just like this necklace, broken and in need of mending. But I don't know if we can mend, girls. I don't know if we can do it. I came here on a fluke. I didn't even know where I was going, but when Dane, that man I had called a friend"—she added bitterly—"told me that I had to leave our house, and only had an hour to pack, I didn't know where to go. I didn't know what to do. So I drove, and then I landed here and walked into the lighthouse and felt the magic of this place."

She ran her hand along the tile floor and sat back, looking up at the plaster ceiling. She sighed and lifted the sapphire up to the light, marveling at how the light pierced the darkness of the stone, nearly turning it an entirely different color.

What a metaphor for life. All a person needed was a bit of light and they would glow, just like that stone.

"So I bought it," she continued as her daughters silently retrieved the pieces of the necklace. "I bought it because I had spent over twenty years doing what your father wanted me to. He never wanted me to cook from that book, so I did. He never thought I could manage much on my own, but I have. He never thought that I could survive without him but look at me. I've done it. I have created a life without Jack Rigby. Oh, I used his money to buy this place, but I'm not using it to keep us going. I'm doing that on my own two feet."

She exhaled, feeling indescribable relief at the ability to finally get all of it out. She felt like her own body was a giant boil that had finally been popped and her truth was coming out whether they liked it or not.

But she should probably explain why she hadn't told them the truth. "Girls, I couldn't tell y'all because I was ashamed."

Reece's expression softened. "Ashamed? What would you have to be ashamed of?"

"I don't know." Ginny lifted her arms and just as quickly dropped them into her lap. "I spent my life with a man who loved another woman, hid her and his child behind my back and then gave them everything that I deserved after he was gone. Can you imagine how everyone must be talking back home? How they must be enjoying that little tidbit of gossip? I can just imagine they all marched over to our house on the pretense of visiting me, but really wanted to meet the new me—the woman who stole my life."

Chandler quietly added, "She probably doesn't even have to shop consignment."

For some reason that made Ginny laugh. The bitter truth of that statement hit home. "I know! She probably doesn't. Savannah's her name. And do you know what else? She didn't even seem ugly and evil, like you would think. She looked young, lost even, like she hadn't asked for any of it."

Chandler scoffed. "But she didn't give it back, did she?"

Ginny laughed. "No, she didn't."

Reece got up and gently handed her sister the broken pieces. "Be right back."

"Where do you think she's going?" Ginny asked when Reece was out of sight.

Chandler shrugged. "Probably to get the superglue."

They stared at each other for a beat before bursting into laughter. "Do you think super glue would work?"

"No," Chandler said flatly.

That made them collapse into another fit of chuckles. A ping went off, and Ginny said, "I think that I heard the microwave."

When Reece returned, she brought with her three paper plates and a covered dish. "Smoked tuna dip," she explained. "I made it myself."

Ginny eyed Chandler. "You hungry?"

"No. But I could eat smoked tuna dip."

Reece handed out crackers, and Ginny didn't bother with a plate. She shoveled her cracker straight into the dip and popped it into her mouth. The heavy smoky flavor mingled with the delicate taste of the fish, creating a symphony of delight in her mouth.

"Oh, Reece," she said with a moan. "You need to be baking and cooking. You don't need to be in medical school. You need to be here, with me. Or someone else's kitchen," Ginny quickly added.

Reece finished her bite of food. "I know. I don't need to be there, and I'm sorry that I didn't tell you."

"I'm not the only person keeping secrets." Ginny chewed another heavenly bite. "For some reason that makes me feel better."

The woman laughed again.

Reece spoke again. "I just felt like I had to finish medical school, you know? For Daddy. But now I'm not so certain. Not after hearing what he did to you, Mama. Correction, *to us*. He didn't just cheat on you. He cheated on his entire family. He stole the honesty from our relationship and tainted the truth."

Ginny's chest clenched in worry. "As hard as this may be to understand, another reason why I didn't want to tell y'all is because I didn't want you to see your father differently. I wanted you to remember him for the good times, for when he was a great father. Reece"—her daughter looked up from the dip and into her mother's eyes—"I'm so sorry. I always thought medical school was your dream. I didn't realize that it was your father's. Ugh. That makes me think there are other things that I don't know. Is there anything else that y'all are keeping from me?"

She looked at Chandler, who shrugged. "Y'all know all my secrets. Hudson and I broke up and I've got my muse back. I just...wonder if we'll get back together."

Ginny squeezed her shoulder. "Only time will tell."

She nodded sadly. "And if it doesn't work out, that's okay. I've reclaimed my muse in Sugar Cove. Mama," she said slowly as if trying to pick every word perfectly. "I know what brought you here wasn't what you wanted. It wasn't what any of us wanted. But it seems like we've each found what we needed to. I know now that living in the city full-time wasn't fueling me creatively, it was sucking the life from me. This place, this beach, seeing the life that exists all around, that's my true muse. No, I don't want to lose Hudson, and I feel bad because he's been writing me letters."

"Shut up," Reece said.

Chandler nodded and Ginny couldn't help but notice the tinge of embarrassment blooming crimson on her cheeks. She opened her purse and pulled out an envelope. "He has been. I always joked with him that Hudson barely had time to text. But here he is, writing letters."

"*Love* letters," Reece teased.

"Yes, basically. He wants to work things out."

Ginny brushed cracker crumbs from her lap. "Girls, if there's one lesson that I've learned in these past few months, it's that you need to embrace honest love and that life isn't worth living in misery. Not that I was miserable with your father. I wasn't, and I wouldn't give y'all up for the world. But what I mean is, you've got to carve your own path, and this isn't Hudson's life to live for you. It's yours, Chandler." Ginny took her hand. "And it's yours, Reece." She took her other daughter's hand. "Y'all only have one shot. You've got to make of it the best that you can, and if true love is waiting for you, you'd better grab ahold of it and hug it tight."

Chandler nodded. "I will, Mama."

"And Reece," she said sharply.

Worry sparked in her youngest daughter's eyes. "Yes?"

"Don't ever do something for someone else if it isn't what you want. You've spent your entire life living the life that your daddy wanted for you. It's time for you to live your own."

A single tear dripped down Reece's cheek. "I will, Mama."

Ginny's grip on her daughters' hands tightened. "Promise me."

"We promise," they told her.

She released their hands. "Now, come here."

Ginny embraced both her girls, feeling a warmth spread out from her chest and down her entire body. Oh, how she wished that she'd confessed the truth to them sooner. But in life, circumstances unwound at the right moment, and she knew that this was that time.

She inhaled deeply and rose. "Chandler, do you think the necklace can be repaired?"

Her daughter studied the broken pieces cupped in her hands. "I can start over, and now it will go quicker because I know how to make it."

"That's a relief," Reece said, exhaling a gusty sigh. "And I'll help you if I can."

"Thank you," Chandler told her, sounding like she meant it.

Ginny's heart was full.

The three women lifted themselves from the floor and had just finished brushing crumbs and dust from their clothes when a knock sounded at the front door.

"Who's that?" Reece said, sounding annoyed as only she could do in her endearing way.

Ginny moved to answer it. "Maybe it's Aiden. He may have left something."

But when she opened the door, it wasn't Aiden she stared up at.

"Hudson?" she said in surprise.

He looked the worse for wear. His curly locks were disheveled, his brown sports coat wrinkled, as was the blue button down beneath it.

Sorrow overflowed in his brown eyes. "Is Chandler here?"

She appeared beside Ginny. "I'm here."

His head dropped in relief. "Do you have time to talk?"

Ginny squeezed Chandler's hand, silently wishing her daughter strength for whatever was about to happen between her and Hudson.

She gave her mother a slight smile in return and said simply, "I'll be back," before slipping from the door and into the night with Hudson by her side.

CHAPTER 39
Chandler

They sat under the full moon on the deck in thickly hewn Adirondack chairs and stared into the lapping waves while listening to the surf crash against the shore.

They hadn't spoken since Chandler had led him to this spot. The lighthouse was surprisingly insulated. You couldn't hear anyone outside, and from the outside, you weren't privileged to eavesdrop on someone hidden behind the brick and mortar of the old building.

"Hudson, what are you doing here?" She tried to make herself sound impartial, impassive, but Chandler knew that the moment that the words flew from her mouth that they sounded harsh and judgmental. She sighed and decided to start over. "What I mean is—"

"What am I doing here?"

He tipped his head toward her, and she immediately felt the pull of his inky eyes and wanted to trace her finger down the line of his jaw and press her nose to the spot just under his neck that always smelled of him —of leather and musk.

She swallowed a hard knot that was stealing all the space in her throat. "Yes, I guess that is what I mean."

"I wrote you letters."

"I got them."

He nodded and stared out into the water. It killed her for him to look away like he had. She wanted to fall into his eyes and never leave. Her chest ached when he turned his head because Hudson was her sun, and when he looked at her, the world opened. When he didn't, the world became a place full of wilted weeds.

She realized then that she needed him as much as she needed her art, this beach, this lighthouse, this town. She *ached* for Hudson in a way that she'd never known. Oh, Chandler had attempted to ignore it, but a person couldn't deny the truth when it stared at them so boldly. This truth—that she yearned for him like air—filled her.

"Did you read them? The letters?" he asked.

"Yes," she confessed. "They were beautiful."

He rapped his fingers on the arm of the chair, and Chandler began to wonder if he'd flown all this way to simply ask about the letters. He could've texted her if that was the case.

Then, as if reading her mind, he said, "You wouldn't have answered if I'd simply texted you. I wanted you to know how I felt, how much you mean to me. Chandler—"

He took her hand then and she let him, savoring the feel of his skin, the calluses on his fingertips, the firm yet gentle way that he held her, as if she was made of porcelain and would break.

Well, she would not, and she knew that now.

"Yes?" she answered, willing him to continue, her eyes searching him, wanting him to give her an opening so that she could tell him how terribly she'd missed him and how she never should have pushed him away.

"I've done some soul searching and realized that if you felt you had to live up to some standard in order to be with me, well, I must've given you that idea to begin with." His voice filled with anger. "I've never wanted you to feel like you weren't good enough, because you are. You are so much better than anyone else I've ever met. My family might have talent, we might be high achievers, but that doesn't mean I don't understand when someone is suffering—which you were. I wish..." He curled his hand into a fist and tapped it against the chair. "I wish that I could've said more to convince you otherwise."

The hurt, the pain in his voice made her heart shrink, made Chandler feel so tiny and silly for what she'd thought. How could she have ever questioned that Hudson would accept her exactly the way that she was?

His jaw flexed in frustration. "I know you. I love you. Being apart from you has nearly destroyed me. I can't work. I barely eat. I don't sleep." He laughed bitterly and the ocean broke against the sand as if echoing his emotion. "My love for you is not wrapped up in your art or who you are professionally. Yes, that's part of it, but not all of it."

He sat up, fully facing her, and laced his fingers together atop his parted knees. "I don't care what you need to do for your art. I want you to be happy. I want you to feel fulfilled. That's all I've ever wanted." He inhaled sharply and stared into the ocean. "My mother has never wanted to be more than a mom and someone who helps charities. She came from nothing. She wasn't high society, and no one ever questioned that she wasn't good enough because my father chose and loved her. She never became a lawyer, but she does good for the charities that she supports. My family loves you, Chandler. All they've ever wanted is for you to succeed."

He whipped his head toward the sand and the beach, drinking in the moonlight as Chandler drank in his beautiful profile that made her heart sing.

These were the words that she had longed to hear, that she desperately needed to know. Hudson didn't care about how successful she was, though having a career was important to her, and it wasn't something that she was going to give up anytime soon. But he wanted to be with her, and she wanted to be with him.

"And so?" she prodded.

"And so." His lips quirked into that lopsided smile that made her heart somersault. He took her hands. "And so, I want us to be together."

"But your job is in New York."

He frowned. "Are you staying here?"

A new wall was thrown up between them. She hadn't come this far, worked so hard on her craft to simply leave it behind.

She mustered up her strength and said, "Yes, I've found my inspiration here. This place, Sugar Cove, it's changed my art. I'm becoming the artist that I was meant to be. And I've been so unfair to you." Tears dripped from her eyes. "I needed to understand myself, so I broke up with you. Yet here you are, and all I want is *you*, and to remain here, in this place. But I can't ask more from you, Hudson, because you've already given me so much. It's my turn to give something back to you." She sighed. "I love you, and I want you to be happy. Your life isn't here, and I could never ask you to change that. Maybe we could do long distance and visit one another."

"That's only a temporary solution," he said.

His eyes darkened and her heart shrank. They were at an impasse. Hudson couldn't leave New York, not with his job, and Chandler didn't want to return. She'd already thought everything out. She'd listed her studio and already had someone willing to rent from her. She only needed to return to pack up her things.

Hudson watched the waves dance in the moonlight. His lips parted and this was it. He would tell her that it wouldn't work out. All their heartache would have been for nothing. He would have poured his heart out, traveled all this way just to leave in defeat.

But that wasn't what he said. Instead he surprised her with, "But if you'd told me sooner, I could've put in for a transfer."

Her heart jolted out of its misery. "What?"

A slow smile curled on his face. "We have an office in the Panhandle. I can transfer down here. Of course, I'll have to be licensed in Florida and that'll take some time, but nothing is impossible."

Chandler couldn't believe what she was hearing. "You're saying...what?"

He rose and pulled her to him until their chests were pressed together and their noses practically touching. Hudson wound his finger around one of her loose hairs and tucked it behind her ear.

"I'm saying"—he kissed the tip of her nose—"that I can move here. If this is where you find joy, I want to share that with you." His lips brushed her cheek. "The only thing I want is to never be apart from you again."

His lips found hers then, and Chandler let him kiss her. It was a kiss filled with longing, of regret for time lost, of hope for a future.

When they parted, Hudson smoothed a hand down her hair and whispered into her lips, "I only wish that I'd come sooner. You are welcome in my family, Chandler. Everyone loves you. All of us."

She quirked a teasing brow. "And you?"

"*Especially* me. I have so much love for you that I don't know how to contain it. I would travel to the ends of the earth for you, and only you."

Her heart swelled again, and they kissed. Hudson pulled her to him, squeezing her tight, but it wasn't tight enough for her.

It was then, from her pocket, that a crunching sound came.

Hudson pulled back. "What is that?"

"Oh." Embarrassment burned her cheeks. "It's a necklace I made. Well, was a necklace. It broke."

His features fell. "Oh no."

She shrugged because it was okay. "I can fix it."

"May I see?"

"Sure." She pulled the shattered fragments of chain and sapphires from their neatly tucked-away spot in the depths of her pocket. "Here."

Hudson studied the fragments, lifting the jewels to the moonlight and turning them over. "I can't wait to see this after you've fixed it."

A grin invaded her face. It was so wide that her cheeks ached from attempting to contain it. "You can definitely see it. When are you moving?"

Hudson threw back his head and laughed. "How does next week sound?"

She tipped her chin up and let him kiss her one more time. "It doesn't sound soon enough."

CHAPTER 40

Reece

The next day Reece called Tulane's Office of the University Registrar and officially unenrolled. It pained her to do it, but it was the right decision and one that she'd needed to perform for weeks.

When the call ended, she pulled the pen from her purse, the one that her father had given her, and tucked it into her apron.

"You might not ever be used to write prescriptions, but you can create recipes that will bring people joy. Sorry, Daddy, but you lived your life doing what you wanted, and so will I."

That had been the final nail in her decision. Jack Rigby had been a liar, and so Reece, though grief-ridden that he was gone, did not feel indentured to live the life that he had carved out for her. She didn't even feel the tiniest tinge of guilt with the decision. In fact, it was quite the opposite. She felt completely at peace.

It was time to start living the life that she wanted, not someone else's.

And so, when she arose in the yawning hours of the morning to twist dough and beat cake batter, she felt unbridled joy in doing so. In fact, she'd baked a surprise for her mother, one that she hoped would bring her comfort and delight.

"What's this?" her mother said when she arrived in the kitchen later that morning and spotted the sheet cake cooling on the counter.

"Coca-Cola cake," Reece replied over her shoulder. She had just brought cocoa powder, Coca-Cola, butter and powdered sugar to a boil on the stove. She stirred it quickly and lifted the pot, beelining for the counter. "Stand aside, Mama. Hot frosting coming through."

Her mother moved out of the way, and Reece quickly poured the hot frosting atop the cake. It spread like chocolate lava, filling in all the cracks at the edges of the pan.

"May I?" Ginny asked, holding a silicone spatula and practically drooling at the cake.

"Go for it." She placed the hot pot back on the stove for it to cool. "I made it for you."

"I couldn't possibly eat all of this," Her mother teased as she smoothed the frosting until it looked like someone had laid a chocolate blanket atop the cake. "But I would be happy to share it."

She laughed. "This is a thank you."

Ginny licked frosting from the spatula, closed her eyes and moaned. "Just like my grandmother used to make. Delicious. Want some?"

Reece scraped her finger along the side of the spatula and popped the warm frosting into her mouth. Sweet chocolate exploded on her tongue. You could just barely taste the Coke, but there was enough of a hint that it sparkled in the background.

"That is so good," Reece agreed.

Ginny paused in her licking. "What do you mean, you wanted to thank me?"

"For understanding all my stupid choices."

"Honey," she said in a voice thick with sympathy, "I don't want you to ever feel like you can't come to me, okay?"

"Okay." Reece smiled at her mother, and her mother smiled back. "I promise."

"Good." Ginny finished licking the spoon. "Now come on. We've got a lunch service to prepare for."

The rest of that morning whizzed by for Reece. For the past few days she'd done everything in her power to not think about Ted and had been successful for the most part. The most part being her mother's discovery of her lack of enrollment at Tulane.

But now that reality was settling in, Reece missed seeing him jog by in the mornings. She missed their casual flirtations. She missed coyly suggesting he eat sweets and him bashfully declining.

She missed the interaction.

The thought made her chest tighten. But when she did get depressed about it, she forced herself to focus on her friendship with Shelby and how she had a good friend in her, someone she could confide in.

And her relationship with Chandler was strengthening, too. After she and Hudson had talked the other night, Chandler came back to their room and told Reece everything that had happened, and that he would be moving to Sugar Cove.

Reece had been overjoyed. Not only because Chandler had given her a piece of herself, but also she was genuinely happy for her sister.

And that joy was what Reece was feeling when the first seating of the lunch crowd poured through the doors of the lighthouse café to enjoy a hearty bowl of shrimp and sausage gumbo packed with okra, and to finish it off with a square of Coca-Cola cake.

She hadn't expected to look up and see Ted walking in holding the hand of a little girl. She hadn't expected to guide him to a table and grab a glass of milk for the girl (who was adorable, by the way, with a constellation of freckles dancing over her nose and eyes the color of sea glass) and an unsweetened iced tea for Ted.

She hadn't expected to feel her heart seize when she brought out their food and the little girl slurped down the gumbo and declared it delicious.

And lastly, she hadn't expected to find herself lingering at their table when she delivered a slice of cake to each of them.

The little girl dug her fork into the cake like a shovel and gobbled the bite with the same gusto.

"This is amazing," she declared.

Reece smiled. "I'm so glad that you like it."

Ted sat back and smiled at her. "Hadley, meet my friend Reece. Reece, this is Hadley."

With perfect manners Hadley said, "How do you do, Miss Reece?"

She grinned from ear to ear at the girl's impeccable Southern charm. "Why, I do just fine. How about you?"

"I'm great," Hadley declared.

She noticed the look of love that Ted gave his daughter. His gaze darted to her, and Reece's cheeks flushed red, embarrassed that he'd caught her staring at him.

"You finally decided to try out the restaurant," she teased.

"I also finally decided to have a sweet." He took a bite, and his eyes popped wide with surprise. "Why, I would have to say this is the best Coca-Cola cake that I've ever tasted."

"Have you ever even had Coca-Cola cake? We both know you're not one to indulge."

"How do you know that?" he replied, eyes sparkling with mischief.

She cocked her head. "Because if you did, you would've taken me up on my dozens of offers for a cinnamon roll."

He chuckled and lifted his hands. "Busted! But that doesn't mean I don't enjoy them every now and then."

"This is good, Daddy," Hadley told him. "You should eat more sweets."

"Why would I eat sweets when I *have* a sweet," he replied, brushing a finger down his daughter's cheek.

Reece's heart nearly seized at the show of love. But she yanked her head down from the clouds and wondered just what Ted was doing there.

"So, did you *just* come for the food?"

"Busted again," he told her, dimples peeking out from his cheeks. "I came to see if you're still with that boyfriend of yours."

Her entire body sang at his words. She could feel his question like a whisper of air snaking down her spine and wrapping itself tightly around her. Reece's fingers flexed, she was so ready to jump in and say yes.

But a flash of light from the window snatched her gaze. A car's mirror had reflected the sun directly in her eyes, and as she turned her head to glance back down at Ted, her gaze grazed over the gas station, where she knew Shelby was perched inside, pining for him.

It felt like a giant hand had grabbed hold of her heart and squeezed every drop of life from it, for in that instant Reece was sucked back into reality.

"I'm sorry," she said. "I'm still with him."

She slid the bill on the table, and he took it and rose. He stood within touching distance. Being that close to him took her back to the deserted hallway when it was just the two of them, and how their hands had brushed together, and she had felt chemistry between them ignite.

Now Reece took a step back and cleared her throat in a shoddy attempt at pushing thoughts of Ted from her head. The problem was, every time he was near, her brain fogged up like a windshield in a storm.

But thoughts of Shelby lived inside her head, too, and this time they won out.

He tapped the bill on the table. "Maybe one day you'll have a different answer."

Her heart was on the floor now. It had most certainly popped out of her chest and landed on the tile.

She could only nod rigidly. To keep from looking into Ted's eyes and betraying Shelby by telling him the truth, that there wasn't another man, she focused on Hadley. "It was so nice meeting you."

"It was a pleasure to meet you as well, Miss Reece."

She chuckled. "Bye, now."

Before she could take back everything that she'd said, she spun on her heel and headed back into the kitchen—

Where she nearly crashed into Chandler holding a pitcher of tea. "Watch out!"

Reece scurried out of the way. "Sorry!"

As her sister whizzed by, Ginny sidled up. "Was that him? The guy you like?"

She placed the dirty dishes in her hands into the hot soapy water in the sink. "Was it obvious? Did I act like an idiot?"

"No," her mother told her, setting another dirty dish atop the others. "You simply brightened when you talked to him. He's very handsome. What's his name?"

"It doesn't matter," she muttered as she started to clean the dishes.

Ginny patted her shoulders that were all scrunched from tension. "Everything happens for a reason."

"Yes, it does."

When her mother moved away, Reece sneaked back to the door and peeked out just in time to see Ted pay for their meal and open the door for Hadley. He glanced back into the restaurant one last time as if searching for Reece.

At least that was what she hoped.

She had just turned away to resume dish washing when Chandler burst through the doors waving a newspaper. "Mama, it's out! The review is in. Come look!"

CHAPTER 41

Ginny

Her hands shook as she wiped them on a towel. Chandler rushed up to her with the newspaper clutched in her hands.

"Go on, read it," she told Ginny.

"Is everyone gone?"

Reece answered. "Yep, last person just left. I'll lock the door before anyone thinks they can get a table before we have the second lunch service ready."

She dashed from the kitchen, and Ginny knew that now was the time for her to look at the paper.

But she couldn't. Worry had gripped her heart, so she pushed the pages back at Chandler. "You read it."

She frowned. "No. It should be you. You put everything into this place, into making it what it is. You deserve to read it."

Ginny, realizing that climbing the lighthouse ladder was more frightening than reading a newspaper article—whether it be good or bad—unclutched her clawed fingers and took hold of the edition that her daughter pressed into her hands.

"Here goes nothing," she announced just as Reece skidded back into the kitchen. "Everyone ready?"

"Oh, I am so ready," her youngest said in a voice that made Ginny smile.

"Me too. Go on," Chandler prodded. "No matter what that man says, I know that this place is worth more than its weight in salt."

Ginny inhaled deeply and placed the paper on the counter. There, splashed on the front page, was the article.

Did the Lighthouse Café Light Up My Tastebuds? by Reynold Thompkins.

From the clapboard sign that announces that the first lunch seating is at 11am to the whiteboard displaying the menu (which changes daily), everything about the Lighthouse Café in Sugar Cove is unique.

Ginny Rigby, owner and creator of the comfort food the café offers, gets her recipes from her grandmother's old cookbook, Magnolia Sisters, *which this reviewer's grandmother has a recipe in.*

I remember that cookbook fondly. When I was a boy, my mother would scour the pages looking for ways to use up day-old fish and scraps of meat.

When Ginny Rigby informed me that she would be cooking my grandmother's chicken and dumplings, aptly titled Ethel's Chicken and Dumplings, I admit that I had high hopes.

No one could cook dumplings like my grandmother.

I arrived promptly at 11am for the first seating and was only asked what I would be drinking, which was sweet tea. The chicken and dumplings arrived promptly. What I saw immediately took me back to my grandmother's kitchen.

Thick chunks of chicken swam in a sturdy broth beneath strips of white dumplings. The smell wrapped me in comfort. This was the dish that Grandmother fixed at Christmas and Easter. I wanted it to be good. Oh, I did.

And I was not disappointed.

The first bite of this perfectly seasoned dish made me think that Ms. Rigby had somehow managed to raise my grandmother from the grave. Others have tried to make it as well, and most of them have failed, save for Ms. Rigby.

The dish was an absolute delight, as was the dessert, homemade banana pudding.

In a coastline dotted with barbecue, seafood and Italian restaurants, Ms. Rigby's home-cooked meals are a welcome addition. Her cooking show-

*cases what makes the South unique and wonderful, and I, for one, wish Ms.
Rigby and the Lighthouse Café many years of success in our small town.*

Ginny's mouth dropped as she finished reading. Reynold Thompkins
had given her a starred review. He hadn't hated the chicken and
dumplings as she had feared. He had loved them! He had adored them.
The dish had transported him back to his grandmother's kitchen, a place
she assumed was full of love and comfort, as her own grandmother's
kitchen had been for her.

Chandler ran her finger down the side of the article as she read it and
tapped it on the last word. "Mama, you've done it! He loved it!"

Her oldest daughter pulled Ginny into a hug, which she welcomed.
Reece hooted and hollered as well, delighted at the news.

"We've got to frame it," Reece announced. "Frame it and hang it up
right inside the front door."

Ginny felt her brow wrinkle with hesitation. "Do you think so?"

"Absolutely," she told her. "I'll run down to the dollar store. I'll be
back in ten minutes."

And fifteen minutes later, only moments before the café opened for
the second lunch seating, Ginny hung the framed article on the wall,
right next to the door so that everyone who entered could read the
review. Or not read it. It didn't matter to her. What did matter was that
her heart was full.

The phone rang as the second seating began. "Lighthouse Café," she
said in answer.

"Have you read it yet?" She instantly recognized Molly's voice on the
other end. "The article that Reynold wrote about you?"

"I have," Ginny gushed. "I framed it and put it on the wall."

"I'm so proud of you," Molly told her. "You've come to Sugar Cove
and made a successful business. I brag to everyone I talk to about your
place, and now even more people will know how wonderful it is. Well
done."

"Thank you, Molly. Let's meet up soon, okay?"

"Yes, let's do that."

She hung up and was quickly catapulted back into work as customers
looking for a table streamed through the front door. Ginny was on her

feet and busy until the last person left, and they locked the door for the day.

She sighed with happiness and made her way into the kitchen to clean up.

Today had been a great day. Could their days at Sugar Cove get any better than that?

CHAPTER 42

Chandler

I t was several weeks later, which wasn't that interesting all in itself except for one thing—Hudson was moving to Sugar Cove.

He'd found a small house on stilts to purchase, and the cost of the place had nearly knocked Chandler onto her rear end. Beachfront real estate prices were sky-high. But Hudson could afford it.

His furniture had been shipped, and they'd just unloaded the last box when Hudson grabbed her by the hand.

"Come here, I want you to see this."

"See what?"

Mischief flashed in his warm brown eyes. "Just come here."

He tugged her to the sliding door that led to the back deck. The sun was beginning to set, and the sky was smeared in pink and smoky purple.

"This," he announced, "is where I want to be every evening. Watching this sunset, sitting out here."

It was glorious, she admitted to herself. Everything about it was beautiful. From the waves crashing along the beach to the salty air, to the colors that stretched out along the horizon, hugging the water.

He sat in a cushioned chair and pulled her onto his lap. "Thank you," he said, gently tugging her down for a kiss.

"For what?" she asked when they parted.

"For making me realize that even though my profession is important, you are more important. Chandler, there's—"

Her phone rang from her purse. Vicki was supposed to call about a potential buyer for some pieces that Chandler had created.

She tapped Hudson's nose. "Hold that thought." She slipped into the kitchen and thumbed her phone to life. "Hello?"

"Chandler, it's Vicki."

"Oh, hi."

"I'm calling because I wanted to let you know that the pieces you showed me the other day are beautiful and I would like to display them in the shop."

Chandler sucked air. "Display them? To sell?"

"Yes. They're remarkable and I know they would fetch a great price. You shouldn't be selling them online. You need a jewelry gallery for your work. I have one. Use my extra space."

Surprise wrapped itself so tightly around her spine that it took her a moment to reply, "Thank you."

She could practically hear the smile in Vicki's voice. "You're welcome. You deserve it."

They said goodbye, and she returned to the deck. "Who was that?" Hudson asked.

She hugged the phone to her chest. "Vicki. She wants to showcase my work in her store."

He took her hand and tugged her back onto the arm of the chair. "That's great. I'm proud of you."

She was proud of herself, too, so much so that her chest swelled. Chandler turned her face to the sunset, and her eyes drank in the warm pinks and rich smears of gold. This was the life. She had Hudson here, her mother's business was flourishing, Reece had even settled down. This was what they all needed.

"Chandler?"

She dragged her face from the sunset to Hudson, who now held a velvet box in his hands. Her heart bounced around in her chest.

He opened the box and there sat a brilliant watermelon tourmaline, her favorite stone, surrounded by diamonds.

"Chandler Rigby, I don't ever want to be without you again. Will you marry me?"

CHAPTER 43

Ginny

S he stood at the very top of the stairs. It was warmer up here than it was down below, at the entrance. Ginny ran her hand along the rough bricks and let their coolness seep into her hand.

Her face burned. Her heart jumped.

She stood before the iron ladder, the one that led up into the top of the lighthouse, where she knew if she could just climb her way up, she would be witness to the most glorious view of her town and the ocean.

Jack's voice whittled away inside her head. *You can't be anything but a housewife. Your place is beside me. I'm the one who takes risks, Ginny. Not you.*

But that wasn't true any longer. She had taken many risks to be where she was, and she had flourished.

Ever so slowly she took the bars of the ladder in her hands, and she lifted her right leg, dropped her foot onto the rung and exhaled.

Okay, she'd made one move toward the climb.

She brought her left foot up and hoisted herself up a notch. That was easy. She'd done it. She climbed again and now her head was parallel with the tiny hole that she had to shimmy through. But it would be worth it. She could conquer this claustrophobia. All she had to do was squeeze her eyes shut—no! Keep them open. She had come this far. She would open her eyes and experience every moment. Every second was worth cherishing, she knew that now.

As she climbed, her heart ticked up, sweat sprouted on her hands, but Ginny ignored it. Instead she focused on her goal, on what her reward would be when she reached the top.

One foot, another foot, lift her hand...she was almost through the hole—

She burst through to the top and exhaled. The inside of the lamphouse was painted white. A glass bulb rested just above her head. She climbed the last steps and hoisted herself onto the ledge. Then she pulled her legs over and stood.

Her breath was shaky, but as her gaze scoured the landscape, she exhaled a strong, stoic breath.

The ocean waves crashed along the beach. Beachgoers walked the shores. A little girl picked up a seashell and raced toward her mother, holding it up proudly.

Behind her, people walked the road that ran along the front of the lighthouse. Tourists rode their bikes, a seafood truck was parked in a lot and a man had just been handed a bag of what would probably become his supper.

Why, Ginny wondered, had she waited so darn long to come up here and experience this? It had been easy once she'd conquered her fear. And now, she realized, she might like to come up every day, maybe put a chair up there, bring binoculars so that she could see what kind of shells the beachcombers had scavenged.

Then a thought struck her. She'd forgotten that Aiden had left her a note. What glee! She laughed at how she'd thought that never would she be retrieving it. It would remain up here a century before anyone ever found it.

She skimmed her hand along the brick until she spotted the small nook that he'd described. The paper poked out, and she pulled it from its home and slowly unfolded it, curiosity leaping in her chest.

What could Aiden have written? What message did he think to give her?

She opened it and her gaze slowly scrolled over his words.

Ginny, when you have the courage to find this note, you will also find the courage to move on.

She leaned back against the glass and considered it and realized that he was right. She did have the courage to move on.

She slipped her hand into her pocket and pulled out her phone. He answered on the first ring.

"I hear you got some good news by way of Reynold Thompkins."

She laughed as she pressed her back onto the outer glass. "You read it?"

"Had to. It talked about my favorite restaurant."

"Your favorite, huh?"

"Absolutely. Best food this side of the Panhandle."

"I thank you for that."

"You're welcome."

Her gaze roved over the lighthouse. "You won't believe where I'm standing."

"Outside my door?"

"No! I'm at the top of the lighthouse."

"You don't say."

"I do, and I read your note."

Silence stretched out between them for a moment before he squashed it single-handedly with, "So. When are you free for a real date?"

She smiled so hard her cheeks ached. Better her cheeks than her heart, she thought. "You sure you want to date me? I'm pretty much a mess. Still reeling from everything that happened with Jack."

"Ginny, I wouldn't have you any other way. Knew that the first moment I saw you and convinced you to bid on the lighthouse."

"You did?"

"Oh yeah. I knew it. Now. What about dinner tomorrow?"

She couldn't help herself. The old Ginny wanted to be reserved, to say no, she couldn't. But this was footloose-and-fancy-free Ginny, so she said, "That sounds great."

They talked a few more minutes, and as soon as she hung up, Reece's voice drifted up from the bottom of the lighthouse.

"Mom! Dinner's ready. Everybody's here—that means Chandler and Hudson."

Everyone, she thought. How wonderful it sounded that her family was downstairs waiting to have supper together.

Ginny took one last look at the horizon, drinking in the brushed strokes of color, and knew that she was home.

"Mom! Where are you?" Reece shouted.

She slipped her phone into her pocket along with the note, curled her hand around the top rung of the ladder and answered, "Up here. In the tower. I'll be down in a second."

She sat down at the opening and glanced around at the boards and glass. Her gaze skimmed over a board that was just barely poking out from the wall. She pressed a hand to smooth it and felt the board spring back.

It seemed like something was there. Ginny reached to the board and pulled it back slightly. Hidden behind it was what appeared to be a small leather-bound book.

She tugged it out, wondering if this was one more thing Aiden had forgotten to tell her about. But when she opened it, the name inside surprised her.

Written in looping handwriting at the very top edge were the words, *Emma Grace's Diary.*

Ginny's body went numb. This was *her* diary. It belonged to the girl who had gone out to the sea to find her lover after his father's boat had crashed onto the rocks.

What story could this diary possibly hold?

"Girls," she called down, "you'll never believe what I found!"

* * *

Thank you for accepting an ARC of The Lighthouse Cafe! I appreciate you taking the time to read my book.

If you'd like to share buy links with your followers, here they are:

Amazon US: https://bit.ly/3KfFAQZ

Amazon UK: https://amzn.to/3Zjkaa1

Amazon CA: https://amzn.to/40q2KcU

Amazon AU: https://amzn.to/3G0Xp3A

Printed in Great Britain
by Amazon

30497696R00128